A Century of
Children's Baseball Stories

A Century of Children's Baseball Stories

Edited by
Debra A. Dagavarian

Stadium Books

Library of Congress Cataloging-in-Publication Data

A Century of children's baseball stories / edited by Debra A.
Dagavarian.
    p.   cm.
    Summary: A collection of baseball stories from the last 100 years.
    ISBN 0-9625132-0-2 (alk. paper) : $
      1. Baseball—Juvenile fiction. 2. Children's stories, American.
  [1. Baseball—Fiction. 2. Short stories.] I. Dagavarian, Debra
A., 1952–
  PZ5.C3   1990
  [Fic]—dc20   89-13554
                                            CIP
                                            AC

British Library Cataloguing in Publication Data

A Century of children's baseball stories.
  I. Dagavarian, Debra A.
  813′.01′08355[J]

  ISBN 0-9625132-0-2

Stadium Books, distributed by the Talman Company, Inc.,
  150 Fifth Avenue, New York, NY 10011

Printed on acid free paper.
Printed and bound in the United States of America.

To my husband, Jim Bonar

Contents

Introduction

"If you never do another thing, my boy, *swat that ball!*," a teammate yells to Marty Brown in Ralph Henry Barbour's 1902 story. Life depended on making that clutch hit, on driving in that run for your teammates, on saving the game for your team. Mere batboys and rookies became heroes. Team spirit drove motley squads to turn plays with finesse. The world of children's baseball built character and taught valuable lessons. It was in this world that little Marty Brown, the town team's good luck charm, got his momentary chance to play alongside the older boys, and contribute to the team effort.

The stories in this book were published in the children's periodicals *American Boy, Boys' Life, The Open Road,* and *St. Nicholas.* Children's writers, typically, are interested in socializing their readers into positive, upright values. Do children's baseball stories, then, allow for certain lessons to be learned? Perhaps so.

Inherent in the game of baseball itself is democracy, as in the taking of one's turn at bat in a fixed order. Interdependence, too, is built into the game of baseball.

Introduction

Pitchers depend upon their batterymates to signal for the right pitches, and make both the routine and the difficult catches. They depend on their fielders to support their efforts in a strong defense. Baserunners rely on teammates to bat them in. A wise catcher, often in control of the pace of the game, will slow down if he sees his pitcher suffering, or will go to the mound if his pitcher needs a moment's pause. Baseball, in almost every sense, encourages supportiveness and cooperation. All this is part of what makes baseball unique and sets it apart from other sports.

My interest in children's baseball stories grew out of a lifelong love of our national pastime. About ten years ago I was given a copy of Lawrence Ritter's *The Glory of Their Times*. Reading the accounts of baseball's early days from the players themselves opened my eyes to the many whimsical characters who predated Babe Ruth. I soon joined SABR, the Society for American Baseball Research, and discovered thousands of other baseball fanatics who cared as much as I did about Christy Mathewson's three shutouts in the 1905 World Series, Joe Wood's invincibility in 1912, and Joe Jackson's having been duped for a pittance in the 1919 Black Sox nightmare. A SABR convention was baseball-heaven to me, and my first introduced me to Bob Wood, son of the great major league pitcher, Smokey Joe Wood.

Smokey Joe was in his nineties when I met him, but still able to demonstrate a wind up motion or recount an anecdote from his colorful Boston years. I would listen to him for hours, never tiring of his reminiscences of Tris

Introduction

Speaker, Stanley Coveleski, Babe Ruth, and other early-twentieth-century players. Spectators cheered with Boston's Royal Rooters, spitballs were legal, and it was Duffy's Cliff, not the Green Monster, that made for creative defense in Fenway's left field. Joe's father trekked to Alaska in search of gold, while Joe and his friends played with baseballs of rolled twine. As a young teenager, Joe would bicycle eighteen miles to another town to pitch a game, earning five dollars if he won, two-fifty if he lost. Summers were spent out of doors, in streets, on sandlots. Baseball in the first two decades of this century, when Smokey Joe played, came alive for me.

It was soon after my meetings with Joe Wood that I became immersed in baseball literature from its beginnings. For doctoral research, I spent many an hour surrounded by crumbling, dusty, old volumes at the Donnell Library in New York City. The stories I collected and analyzed were the basis of an earlier book, *Saying It Ain't So: American Values As Revealed In Children's Baseball Stories, 1880–1950* (Peter Lang Publishing, Inc., 1987). Several of the best stories discussed in that work appear in this volume.

The oldest story in this book, which also is the first such piece of baseball fiction published, appeared in 1882. "The Captain of the Orient Base-Ball Nine," by C. M. Sheldon, illustrates the importance of honesty. Team captain Gleason appears to have scooped up a fly ball to win the game, but in reality has only trapped it. He wrestles with his conscience. Should he defer to the

Introduction

umpire who earnestly called it an out, basking in the glory of victory? Or should he admit the truth and forfeit the game? Setting the stage for decades of children's baseball stories to come, Charles Monroe Sheldon (1857–1946) uses the medium to convey a message.

Sheldon, author of this heavily moralistic tale, was a former pastor of the Central Congregational Church of Topeka, Kansas. Later in life, Sheldon became editor of *The Christian Herald*. His best known and most influential work was the religious novel *In His Steps* (1896), which is estimated to have sold well over six million copies.

One of the most interesting stories in this collection is William Heyliger's "Hit or Error?" Heyliger was a newspaperman born in Hoboken, New Jersey in 1884. He was quite young when he began his cherished vocation of writing, both stories for boys, and articles for Hoboken's *Hudson Observer*. His short stories heralded a growing sophistication in baseball fiction for children.

"Hit or Error?," written in 1924, finds Jimmy, the school team's official scorekeeper, faced with the difficult decision of how to score a ninth inning infield drive with a no-hit game in progress. With two outs in the ninth, the next batted ball falls into left field after having bounced off the third baseman's glove. Jimmy tries to convince himself that the ball should have been caught and that he would be justified in scoring it an error to preserve the no-hitter for his admired friend, the pitcher. He also is resentful of the third baseman, to whom he had lost that coveted job earlier in the season during team tryouts.

The relative complexity of Jimmy's thought processes and eventual decision is somewhat unusual in early-twentieth-century children's baseball literature. Heyliger's characters show a range of thought and emotion, and are influenced by an array of both internal and external factors. With Heyliger and his contemporaries, children's baseball stories in the twenties had started to become more cosmopolitan.

Before Heyliger, the outstanding children's baseball writer of his time was the prolific Ralph Henry Barbour (1870–1944). Barbour's descriptions of fictional games were so vivid, they were said to have actually influenced the coverage of real games in newspapers. Barbour's own multi-faceted career included newspaper work—as a reporter, correspondent, literary editor, and copy editor. He also spent four years as a Colorado rancher. Whether or not Barbour enlivened sports reporting is open to question, but he undeniably improved the quality of his genre. His fictional characters were well-intentioned little innocents who would overcome the odds or make a heartfelt sacrifice for the good of the team. "Marty Brown—Mascot" is a typically enchanting example of Barbour's never-say-die characterizations.

The most popular theme in children's baseball fiction is interpersonal support. This is the kind of cooperation or teamwork amongst players which often appears between the pitcher and his catcher or the shortstop and second baseman. Each position thrives on the other, and cooperation is necessary for their mutual success.

Batterymates show interpersonal support for one another in Franklin Reck's 1932 gem, "The Strikeout King." Franklin Mering Reck (1896–1965), who also wrote under the name of F. R. Mering, was a writer and editor. This WW I veteran dabbled in trout fishing, camping, cribbage and poker playing, amateur photography, and the ukelele. Reck was managing editor of *American Boy* from 1934 to 1941, and boy's editor for *Farm Journal* later on. Reck shrugged off the prospect of a business school education and attended Iowa State College, where he later became assistant to the President. A champion of causes, Reck, as national president of Sigma Delta Chi in the 1930s, fought for the right of a black student to gain entry to the fraternity against considerable protest, and worked in the steel mills to raise awareness of the problems of steelworkers. He spent his latter years researching and writing about innovative farming methods to stimulate productivity in Latin America.

Reck's own diversity inspires one of the finest baseball tales ever printed. In "The Strikeout King," String, who aspires to pitch in the major leagues, is urged by his catcher, Poke, to slow down. Poke advocates control, while String, emulating his pitching idol, wants only to impress the scouts with his "stuff." When String does not heed Poke's advice, he develops a sore arm. He also discovers his pitching idol is burnt out. String's eventual lesson in humility, his acknowledgment of Poke's support, and the encouraging assessment of his pitching blend for an upbeat finale.

One brief entry from 1979 is "The Game Ball," by A. R. Swinnerton, in which the talented main character yearns for acceptance by his teammates, particularly in the form of a nickname. By a fluke of circumstance, in which his performance is less than dazzling, he earns his nickname and the camaraderie of his teammates. Swinnerton, born in 1912, worked for many years at American Standard, Inc., as a plant buyer. Among his writings for children are a number of magazine contributions and his highly regarded *Rocky the Cat* books (Addison-Wesley, 1981, 1982). Swinnerton is a kind gentleman who currently lives in northern Ohio.

"Bunt," published in 1980 by Mary Fantina, highlights the significance of interpersonal support and individual responsibility. Fantina is a technical writer with a Ph.D. in organic chemistry. Her main characters are Bunt and Ex, two veteran major league ballplayers who finally make it to the World Series against the Yankees. Each man has his specialized skills—Bunt always bunts, and Ex gets extra base hits. Clutch hitting, heart, and sacrifice all lead to the interesting twist in this plot. Not only is this a good story—it also is good baseball.

Good baseball exists only within a framework of interpersonal support and individual responsibility. Although these are the most prevalent themes in children's baseball stories, humility, or the humbling realization that one is fallible, also ranks high as a thematic element.

Introduction

John R. Tunis' *The Kid From Thomkinsville*, part of a book-length serial, deals with this theme. In the world of baseball fiction, Tunis (1889–1975) was one of the best. He was born in Boston, educated at Harvard, and lived in Essex, Connecticut. Before becoming a writer, he had been a sportswriter and radio sportscaster. Tunis is fondly remembered by many adults today who, as youngsters, read his sports stories with pleasure. Reading this story as an adult should be a special treat.

This portion of *The Kid From Thomkinsville* appeared in *The Open Road*, and is strong enough to stand on its own. It is about a rookie pitcher for the Dodgers who impresses everyone with his talent, but makes some "bonehead" moves (such as forgetting the number of outs while on base and destroying a rally). Roy learns humility, and through the spirited support of his teammates, is redeemed.

The major leagues are also the backdrop for Jim Brosnan's "Opening Day." Brosnan, a former major leaguer, wrote "Opening Day" about a spring training hopeful's initiation to the bigs. Brosnan, born in 1929, pitched for the Chicago Cubs, St. Louis Cardinals, Cincinnati Reds, and Chicago White Sox from 1954 to 1963. He is a likeable man whose writing ability and reverence for the printed word destined him for a second career in writing.

"Opening Day" is most notable for its realism in banter (within, of course, the bounds of suitability for children) and in the depiction of selective camaraderie between veterans and rookies. Arriving at the spring training camp of a major league team is the talented youngster Tommy. The story follows Tommy through his Floridian initiation and, in the end, finds him somewhat humbled by the realization that "there will be another opening day."

Bill Gutman's "Shortstop" is another tale which emphasizes interpersonal support and team spirit. Dave, new shortstop on his high school's inept team, rues leaving his old school's talented team and glaringly outshines his teammates. His big league aspirations and ballplaying ability alienate him, until he begins coaching his teammates. This has the dual effect of improving the team's playing ability, and redefining Dave as "one of the guys." When Dave ultimately needs the support of his teammates, they are there for him.

Gutman's professional roots, like several other writers' of children's baseball stories, lie in journalism. He spent time as a reporter and feature writer for a newspaper in Connecticut, and later became its sports editor. Most of Gutman's many books are about sports and sports figures, though some are biographies of non-sports professionals.

One important element in children's baseball stories not to be overlooked is the role of the coach. The coach not only is the baseball savant, he is the respected mentor to impressionable youngsters. He represents integrity, and molds the youths into virtuous individuals. He is always trusted and usually obeyed. He is sometimes a hero. He acts solely for the good of the team. In "Hit or Error?," for example, he bursts the would-be third baseman's dream by appointing him scorekeeper. The coach-figure always stands for and teaches the moral good.

Even if the stories themselves teach little or nothing, they are pleasurable to read. Children and adults alike can enjoy their pastoral and sentimental quality. The earlier stories remind us of a bygone era when life, in retrospect, at the very least, seemed simple and basic. Perhaps we seek to bring into our lives some of that innocence, that heartfelt desire to give of oneself for the good of the team, the need to be part of a cooperative effort against a backdrop of fair play.

Good baseball stories continue to be written today, and this bodes well for the genre. There is a renewed interest in baseball overall, as with the production of such movies as *The Natural, Eight Men Out, Bull Durham, Major League,* and *Field of Dreams.* But baseball, and children playing baseball, do not belong to any one time in American history. Children's baseball stories are timeless, a product of the imaginations of writers who love the game. Baseball stories, too, belong to all time, or to no particular time. The same pastoral, almost victorian, quality which permeates the earliest stories, still appears in the latest. Here is one medium in which we, as technologically advanced beings, can take respite. So nestle yourself in a cozy spot and delight in the idyllic world of children's baseball.

The Captain of the Orient Base-Ball Nine

C. M. Sheldon

The Orient Base-ball Nine, of Orient Academy, hereby challenges the Eagles, of Clayton Academy, to a match game of ball; time and place to be at the choice of the challenged.

Respectfully,

Tom Davis, Secretary of Orient B.B.C.

To Secretary of Eagle B.B.C., of Clayton Academy.

"There!" said Tom, as he wiped his pen on his coat-sleeve; "how'll that do?"

The Orient Base-ball nine was sitting in solemn council in Captain Gleason's room. The question had long been debated at the Orient School about playing a match game with the Eagles of Clayton, the rival Academy on the same line of railroad, about thirty miles from Orient. Until lately, the teachers of the Academy had withheld their permission for the necessary absence from school; but at last they had yielded to the petitions of the nine, and the Orient Club was now holding a meeting which had resulted in the above challenge.

"Very well put, Tom," answered Gleason, and then an animated conversation took place.

"We must beat those fellows, or they'll crow over us forever."

"Yes; do you remember, fellows, that Barton who was down here last fall when our nine played the town boys? They say he stole a ball out of Tom's pocket during the game. I hear he's short-stop this year." This from Johnny Rider, the Orient first-baseman.

"We don't know about that," said Gleason. "Don't be too sure."

"Well," put in Wagner the popular catcher of the nine, "we *do* know some of them are not to be trusted, and will cheat, if they get a chance. You see if they don't."

"All the more reason why we should play fair, then," retorted Gleason. "Look here, boys, I have n't time to orate, and am not going to make a speech, but let's understand one another. If we go to Clayton—and I think they will prefer to play on their own grounds—we are going to play a fair game. If we can't beat them without cheating, we wont beat them at all!"

"Three cheers for the captain!" shouted Tom, upsetting the inkstand in his excitement. The cheers were given; and the pitcher, a short, thick-set fellow, with quick, black eyes, whispered to Wagner: "If there's any cheating done, it wont be done by Glea, that's sure."

"No," replied Wagner; "but they will beat us. You mark my words."

"We shall have something to say to that, I think;" and the Orient pitcher shut his teeth together vigorously, as he thought of the latest curve which he had been practicing.

Gradually, after more talk on the merits of the two clubs, one after another dropped out of the captain's room, and at last he and Tom Davis were alone. Tom was sealing up the challenge.

"What do you think, Glea, of Rider's remark about Barton?" asked Tom, as he licked a stamp with great relish. Base-ball was food and drink to Tom.

"Why," replied Gleason, "I don't think Barton's any worse than the others. None of them are popular around here, but I think it's only on account of the jealousy of the two academies. Probably they have the same poor opinion of us."

"They're a good nine, anyway. You know they beat the Stars last Saturday."

"Yes," said Gleason, smiling, "and we beat the Rivals."

"Do you think they'll cheat, or try to?" asked Tom.

"Well, no; there is n't much chance of cheating nowadays at base-ball. We may have some trouble with the umpire."

"Well, good-night, old fellow!" said Tom, as he rose.

"I'll take this down to post, and then hie me to my downy couch. I suppose you are going to 'dig,' as usual?"

"Yes; I have some Virgil to get out."

"I don't envy you. Good-night, my *pius Æneas*."

"Good-night, my *fidus Achates*." And the captain was left alone.

He took down his books, but somehow he could not compose himself to study. The anticipated game with the Claytons filled his mind, and he could think of nothing else; so he shut the books, and took a turn up and down the room.

Young Gleason was a handsome, well-built fellow, with an open, sunny face, the very soul of honor, and a popular fellow with every one. He was all but worshiped by the nine, who adored him as a decided leader, a steady player, and a sure batsman, with a knack of wresting victory out of seeming defeat. His powers of endurance were the wonder and admiration of all the new boys, who were sure to hear of Gleason before they had been in the school two days.

He had whipped Eagen, the bully, in the cotton-mills across the river, for insulting some ladies; he had walked from Centerville to Orient in thirty-six minutes, the fastest time on record; he had won the silver cup at the last athletic tournament, for the finest exhibition of the Indian clubs; and, in short, he was a school hero, and not only the boys but the teachers of the Academy learned to admire and love him.

Perhaps the weakest point in his character was his thirst for popularity. He felt keenly any loss of it, and when Sanders carried off the first prize for original declamation, it was noticed that Gleason treated Sanders rather coldly for some time. But, in spite of this defect, Gleason was a splendid fellow, as every one said, and sure to make his mark in the world along with the best.

For two days the nine waited impatiently for the answer to their challenge. The third day it came. The Claytons, with characteristic coolness, Wagner said, chose their own grounds, and a week from date for the match.

"Should n't wonder at all if they tried to work in some outside fellow for pitcher. I hear their own is a little weak," said the ever-suspicious Wagner.

"I'm glad they've given us a week," said Francis the pitcher. "I need about that time for practice on the new curve, and I think you will need about the same time to learn how to catch it. So stop your grumbling, old boy, and come out on the campus."

The week sped rapidly by, and at last the appointed day arrived—clear, cool, still; just the perfection of weather for ball.

A large delegation went down to the station to see the nine off.

"I say, Glea," shouted a school-mate, "telegraph down the result, and we'll be here with a carriage to drag you up the hill when you come back."

"Yes," echoed another; "that is, if you beat. We can't turn out of our beds to get up a triumphal march for the vanquished."

"All right, fellows—we're going to beat them. We're *sure* to beat them—hey, Captain?" said Tom, looking up at Gleason.

"We'll do our best, boys," answered Gleason. Then, as the train moved off, he leaned far out of his window and whispered impressively: "You may be here with that carriage."

There was a cheer from the students, another from the nine standing on the platform and leaning out of the windows, and the Orients were whirled rapidly off to Clayton.

They reached their destination in little more than an hour, and found almost as large a delegation as they had left at Orient. The talk and excitement here for the past week over the coming game had been as eager as at Orient. Nothing about the visitors escaped the notice of the Claytons. Their "points" were discussed as freely as if they were so many prize cattle at a county fair.

"Just look at that fellow's chest and arms!"

"He'll be a tough customer at the bat, I'm afraid."

"He's the fastest runner at Orient."

These and other whispers drew a large share of the attention to Gleason, and, as usual, admiration seemed to stimulate him to do his best. He summoned the nine together before the game was called, to give them final instructions.

"Keep cool. Play steady. Don't run any foolish risks in stealing bases; and, above all, let every man do honest work. Show these fellows that we know what the word *gentleman* means."

The Captain of the Orient Base-Ball Nine

After some little delay necessary for selecting an umpire and arranging for choice of position, the game was finally called, the Orients coming first to the bat.

The crowd gathered to witness the game was the largest ever seen on the grounds, and almost every man was in sympathy with the home nine. So, as Gleason had said on the train, the only hope of his men for victory was to play together, and force the sympathy of some of the spectators, at least, by cool and steady work.

The captain himself was the first man at the bat. After two strikes he succeeded in getting a base hit, stole to second on a passed ball, reached third on a base hit by Wagner, and home on a sacrifice hit by Davis, scoring the first run for Orient amid considerable applause. The next two batters struck out in quick succession, leaving Wagner on second.

Then the Claytons came to the bat, and after an exciting inning scored two runs, showing strength as batters and base-runners. In the third inning the Orients made another run, thus tying the score.

So the game went on until the ninth and last inning, when the score stood eight to seven in favor of the Orients.

The excitement by this time was intense. The playing all along had been brilliant and even. Both nines showed the same number of base hits and nearly the same number of errors. Francis, for the Orients, had done splendid work, but Wagner for some reason had not supported him as well as usual. And now, as the Claytons came to the bat for the closing inning, every one bent forward, and silence reigned over the field, broken only by the voice of the umpire.

Gleason had played a perfect game throughout. No one looking at him could imagine how much he had set his heart on the game. His coaching had been wise, his judgment at all times good, and he now, from his position in left field, awaited the issue of the closing inning with a cheerful assurance.

The inning opened with a sharp hit to short-stop. He made a fine stop and threw to first, but poor Johnny Rider, who had played so far without an error, muffed the ball, and the Clayton batsman took his first amid a perfect storm of cries and cheers.

The next batter, after a strike, drove the ball into right field, a good base hit, and the man on first took second. Then, as if to aggravate the Orients and complete their nervousness, Francis allowed the third batsman to take first on called balls; and so the bases were filled. A player on every base and no one out! It was enough to demoralize the coolest players.

But Francis was one of those men who, after the first flurry of excitement, grow cooler. The next two Claytons struck out in turn.

Then Barton came to the bat, and all the Orients held their breath, and the Claytons watched their strongest batsman with hope. One good base hit would tie them with the Orients, and Barton had already made a two-bagger and a base hit during the game. The umpire's voice sounded out over the field:

"One ball. Two balls. One strike. Three balls. Four

balls. Five balls. Two strikes." Francis ground his teeth, as he delivered the next ball directly over the plate. But Barton, quick as lightning, struck, and the ball went spinning out above short-stop, between second and third.

It was one of those balls most difficult to catch, nearly on a line, and not far enough up to allow much time for judgment as to its direction. Gleason was standing well out in the field, expecting a heavy drive of the ball there, where Barton had struck before. But he rushed forward, neck or nothing, in what seemed a useless attempt. With a marvel of dexterity and quickness, he stooped as he ran, and, reaching down his hand, caught the ball just as it touched the ground, by what is known in base-ball language as a "pick-up."

He felt the ball touch the ground, heard it distinctly, and knew that, where it had struck, a tuft of grass had been crushed down and driven into the earth; and he had straightened himself up to throw the ball home, when a perfect roar of applause struck his ears, and the umpire declared "out on the fly."

He was just on the point of rushing forward and telling the truth, but, as usual after a game, the crowd came down from the seats with a rush, the Orients came running up to him, declaring it the best play they ever saw; and before he knew what he was about, the nine had improvised a chair and carried him off, with cheers and shouts, to the station, for the game had been so long that they could not stay later, as they had planned.

It certainly was a great temptation. Besides, the umpire had declared it a fly. What right had he to dispute the umpire? And no one but himself knew that the ball had touched the ground. The whole action had been so quick, he had run forward so far after feeling the ball between his fingers, that not the least doubt existed in the minds of the Claytons that the catch was a fair one.

But, on the other hand, his conscience kept pricking him. He, the upright, the preacher to the rest of the nine on fair play, the one who had been such a stickler for the right, no matter what the result, he had been the only one to cheat! Yes, it was an ugly word. Cheat! But he could find no other name for it. And after all he had said!

He sat in silence during the ride home. The rest of the nine made noise enough, and as he was generally quiet, even after a victory, no one noticed his silence very much.

As the train ran into the station at Orient a great crowd was in waiting. Tom had telegraphed the news from Clayton, and all Orient was wild with joy. When Gleason appeared, he received a regular ovation, such an ovation as a school-boy alone can give or receive. They rushed him into the carriage, and before the order was given to pull up the hill to the Academy, some one cried out, "Speech, speech!"

It was the most trying moment of Gleason's life. During the ride home he had fought a battle with himself, more fiercely contested than the closest game of ball, and he had won. He trembled as he rose, and those who stood nearest the lights about the station noticed that his face was pale. There was silence at once.

"Fellows, I have something to tell you which you don't expect to hear. We would n't have won the game to-day if I had n't cheated."

"How's that?"

"Who cheated?"

"What's the matter?"

There was the greatest consternation among the Orients. When quiet had been partly restored, Gleason went on and related the whole event just as it happened. "And now," he concluded sadly, "I suppose you all despise me. But you can't think worse of me than I do myself." And he leaped out of the carriage, and, setting, his face straight before him, walked away up the hill.

No one offered to stop him. Some hissed. A few laughed. The majority were puzzled.

"What did he want to tell for? No one would ever have known the difference."

But Tom Davis ran after the captain, and caught him about half-way up the hill. School-boy fashion, he said never a word, but walked up the hill to the captain's room, shook hands with him at his door, and went away with something glittering in his eyes.

Next morning, Gleason's conduct was the talk and wonder of the whole school. But the captain himself showed true nobility. He begged the school and the nines to consider the game played with the Claytons as forfeited to them. And, after much talk, Gleason himself wrote, explaining the whole affair, and asking for another game on the Orient grounds.

The Claytons responded, came down, and defeated the Orients in a game even more hotly contested than the first. But Gleason took his defeat very calmly, and smilingly replied to Tom's almost tearful, "Oh, why did n't we beat this time?" with, "Ah! Tom, but I have a clear conscience, and that is worth more than all the ball-games in the world!"

Marty Brown— Mascot

Ralph Henry Barbour

M artin—more familiarly "Marty"—Brown's connection with the Summerville Baseball Club had begun the previous spring, when, during a hotly contested game with the High School nine, Bob Ayer, Summerville's captain, watching his men go down like ninepins before the puzzling curves of the rival pitcher, found himself addressed by a small snub-nosed, freckle-faced youth with very bright blue eyes and very dusty bare feet:

"Want me ter look after yer bats?"

"No."

"All right," was the cheerful response.

The umpire called two strikes on the batsman, and Bob muttered his anger.

"I don't want nothin' fer it," announced the boy

beside him, insinuatingly, digging a hole in the turf with one bare toe.

Bob turned, glad of something to vent his wrath upon. "No! Get out of here!" he snarled.

"All right," was the imperturbable answer.

Then the side was out, and Bob trotted to first base. That half inning, the last of the seventh, was a tragedy for the town nine, for the High School piled three runs more on their already respectable lead, and when Bob came in he had well-defined visions of defeat. It was his turn at the bat. When he went to select his stick he was surprised to find the barefooted, freckle-faced youth in calm possession.

"What—?" he began angrily.

Marty leaped up and held out a bat. Bob took it, astonished to find that it was his own pet "wagon-tongue," and strode off to the plate, too surprised for words. Two minutes later, he was streaking toward first base on a safe hit to center field. An error gave him second, and the dwindling hopes of Summerville began to rise again. The fellows found the High School pitcher and fairly batted him off his feet, and when the side went out it had added six runs to its tally, and lacked but one of being even with its opponent. Meanwhile Marty rescued the bats thrown aside, and arranged them neatly, presiding over them gravely, and showing a marvelous knowledge of each batsman's wants.

Summerville won that game by two runs, and Bob Ayer was the first to declare, with conviction, that it was "all owing to Marty. The luck had changed," he said, "as soon as the snub-nosed boy had taken charge of the club's property."

Every one saw the reasonableness of the claim, and Marty was thereupon adopted as the official mascot and general factotum of the Summerville Baseball Club. Since then none had disputed Marty's right to that position, and he had served tirelessly, proudly, mourning the defeats and glorying in the victories as sincerely as Bob Ayer himself.

Marty went to the grammar-school "when it kept," and in the summer became a wage-earner to the best of his ability, holding insecure positions with several grocery and butcher stores as messenger and "special delivery." But always on Saturday afternoons he was to be found squatting over the bats at the ball-ground; he never allowed the desire for money to interfere with his sacred duty as mascot and custodian of club property. Every one liked Marty, and he was as much a part of the Summerville Baseball Club as if one of the nine. His rewards consisted chiefly of discarded bats and balls; but he was well satisfied: it was a labor of love with him, and it is quite probable that, had he been offered a salary in payment of the services he rendered, he would have indignantly refused it. For the rest, he was fifteen years old, was not particularly large for his age, still retained the big brown freckles and the snub nose, had lively and honest blue eyes, and, despite the fact that his mother eked out a scanty living by washing clothes for the well-to-do of the town, had a fair idea of his own importance, without, however, risking his popularity by becoming too familiar. The bare feet were covered now by a pair of run-down and very dusty shoes, and his blue calico shirt and well-patched trousers were always clean and neat. On his brown hair rested, far back, a blue-and-white baseball cap adorned with a big S, the gift of Bob Ayer, and Marty's only badge of office.

To-day Marty had a grievance. He sat on a big packing-box in front of Castor's Cash Grocery and kicked his heels softly against its side. Around him the air was heavy with the odor of burning paper and punk, and every instant the sharp sputter of fire-crackers broke upon his reverie. It was the Fourth of July and almost noon. It was very hot, too. But it was not that which was troubling Marty. His grief sprung from the fact that, in just twenty minutes by the town-hall clock up there, the Summerville Baseball Club, supported by a large part of the town's younger population, would take the noon train for Vulcan to play its annual game with the nine of that city; and it would go, Marty bitterly reflected, without its mascot.

Vulcan was a good way off,—as Marty viewed distance,—and the fare for the round trip was $1.40, just $1.28 more than Marty possessed. He had hinted to Bob Ayer and to "Herb" Webster, the club's manager, the real need of taking him along—had even been gloomy and foretold a harrowing defeat for their nine in the event of his absence from the scene. But Summerville's finances were at low ebb, and, owing to the sickness of one good player and the absence of another, her hopes of capturing the one-hundred-dollar purse which was yearly put up by the citizens of the rival towns were but slight. So Marty was to be left behind. And that was why Marty sat on the packing-case and grieved, refusing to join in the lively sport of his friends who, farther up the street, were firing off a small brass cannon in front of Hurlbert's hardware-store.

Already, by ones and twos, the Vulcan bound citizens were toiling through the hot sun toward the station. Marty watched them, and scowled darkly. For the time he was a radical socialist, and railed silently at the unjust manner in which riches are distributed. Presently a group of five fellows, whose ages varied from seventeen to twenty-one, came into sight upon the main street. They wore gray uniforms, with blue-and-white stockings and caps of the same hues, and on their breasts were big blue S's. Two of them carried, swung between them, a long leather bag containing Marty's charge, the club's bats. The players spied the boy on the box, and hailed him from across the street. Marty's reply was low-toned and despondent. But after they had turned the corner toward the station, he settled his cap firmly on his head and, sliding off the box, hurried after them.

The station platform was well filled when he gained it. Bob Ayer was talking excitedly to Joe Sleeper, and Marty, listening from a distance, gathered that Magee, the Summerville center-fielder, had not put in his appearance.

"If he fails us," Bob was saying anxiously, "it's all up before we start. We're crippled already. Has any one seen him?"

None had, and Bob, looking more worried than before, strode off through the crowd to seek for news. Of course, Marty told himself, he did n't want Summerville to lose, but, just the same, if they did, it would serve them right for not taking him along. A long whistle in the distance sounded, and Bob came back, shaking his head in despair.

"Not here," he said.

A murmur of dismay went up from the group, and Marty slid off the baggage-truck and approached the captain.

"Say, let me go along, won't yer, Bob?"

Bob turned, and, seeing Marty's eager face, forgot his worry for the moment, and asked kindly: "Can you buy your ticket?"

"No." Marty clenched his hands and looked desperately from one to another of the group. The train was thundering down the track beside the platform. "But you fellows might buy me one. And I'd pay yer back, honest!"

"Say, Bob, let's take him," said Hamilton. "Goodness knows if we ever needed a mascot, we need one to-day! Here, I'll chip in a quarter."

"So'll I," said Sleeper. "Marty ought to go along; that's a fact."

"Here's another." "You pay for me, Dick, and I'll settle with you when we get back." "I'll give a quarter, too."

"All aboard!" shouted the conductor.

"All right, Marty; jump on," cried Bob. "We'll find

the money—though I don't know where your dinner's coming from!"

Marty was up the car-steps before Bob had finished speaking, and was hauling the long bag from Wolcott with eager hands. Then they trooped into the smoking-car since the day-coaches were already full, and Marty sat down on the stiff leather seat and stood the bag beside him. The train pulled out of the little station, and Marty's gloom gave place to radiant joy.

The journey to Vulcan occupied three quarters of an hour, during which time Bob and the other eight groaned over the absence of Magee and Curtis and Goodman, predicted defeat in one breath and hoped for victory in the next, and rearranged the batting-list in eleven different ways before they were at last satisfied. Marty meanwhile, with his scuffed shoes resting on the opposite seat, one brown hand laid importantly upon the leather bag and his face wreathed in smiles, kept his blue eyes fixedly upon the summer landscape that slid by the open window. It was his first railway trip of any length, and it was very wonderful and exciting. Even the knowledge that defeat was the probable fate ahead of the expedition failed to more than tinge his pleasure with regret.

At Vulcan the train ran under a long iron-roofed structure, noisy with the puffing of engines, the voices of the many that thronged the platforms, and the clanging of a brazen gong announcing dinner in the station restaurant. Marty was awed but delighted. He carried one end of the big bag across the street to the hotel, his eager eyes staring hither and thither in wide amaze. Vulcan boasted of a big bridge-works and steel-mills, and put on many of the airs of a larger city. Bob told Marty that they had arranged for his dinner in the hotel dining-room, but the latter demurred on the score of expense.

"Yer see, I want ter pay yer back, Bob, and so I guess I don't want ter go seventy-five cents fer dinner. Why, that's more 'n what three dinners costs us at home. I'll just go out and get a bit of lunch, I guess. Would yer lend me ten cents?"

Marty enjoyed himself thoroughly during the succeeding half-hour. He bought a five-cent bag of peanuts and three bananas, and aided digestion by strolling about the streets while he consumed them, at last finding his way to the first of the wonderful steel-mills and wandering about freely among the bewildering cranes, rollers, and other ponderous machines. He wished it was not the Fourth of July; he would like to have seen things at work. Finally, red-faced and perspiring, he hurried back to the hotel and entered a coach with the others, and was driven through the city to the ball-ground. This had a high board fence about it, and long tiers of seats half encircling the field. There were lots of persons there, and others were arriving every minute. Marty followed the nine into a little dressing-room built under the grand stand, and presently followed them out again to a bench in the shade just to the left of the home plate. Here he unstrapped his bag and arranged the bats on the ground, examining them carefully, greatly impressed with his own importance.

The Vulcans, who had been practising on the diamond, trotted in, and Bob and the others took their
places. The home team wore gray costumes with maroon
stockings and caps, and the big V that adorned the
shirts was also maroon. Many of them were workers in
the steel-mills, and to Marty they seemed rather older
than the Summervilles. Then the umpire, a very small
man in a snuff-colored alpaca coat and cap, made his
appearance, and the men at practice came in. The
umpire tossed a coin between Bob and the Vulcans'
captain, and Bob won with "heads!" and led his players
into the field. A lot of men just back of Marty began to
cheer for the home team as Vulcan's first man went to
bat.

It were sorry work to write in detail of the disastrous
first seven innings of that game. Summerville's hope of
taking the one-hundred-dollar purse home with them
languished and dwindled, and finally faded quite away
when, in the first half of the seventh inning, Vulcan
found Warner's delivery and batted the ball into every
quarter of the field, and ran their score up to twelve.
Summerville went to bat in the last half plainly discouraged. Oliver struck out. Hamilton hit to second
base and was thrown out. Pickering got first on balls, but
"died" there on a well-fielded fly of Warner's.

Vulcan's citizens yelled delightedly from grand stand
and bleachers. Summerville had given a stinging defeat
to their nine the year before at the rival town, and this
revenge was glorious. They shouted gibes that made
Marty's cheeks flush and caused him to double his fists

wrathfully and wish that he were big enough to "lick somebody"; and they groaned dismally as one after another of the blue-and-white players went down before Baker's superb pitching. Summerville's little band of supporters worked valiantly against overwhelming odds to make their voices heard, but their applause was but a drop in that sea of noise.

The eighth inning began with the score 12 to 5, and Stevens, captain and third baseman of the Vulcans, went to bat with a smile of easy confidence upon his face. He led off with a neat base-hit past short-stop. The next man, Storrs, their clever catcher, found Warner's first ball, and sent it twirling skyward in the direction of left field. Webster was under it but threw it in badly, and Stevens got to third. The next batsman waited coolly and took his base on balls. Warner was badly rattled, and had there been any one to put in his place he would have been taken out. But Curtis, the substitute pitcher, was ill in bed at Summerville, and helpless Bob Ayer ground his teeth and watched defeat overwhelm him. With a man on third, another on first, and but one out, things again looked desperate.

Warner, pale of face, wrapped his long fingers about the ball and faced the next batsman. The coaches kept up a volley of disconcerting advice to the runners, most of it intended for the pitcher's ear, however. On Warner's first delivery the man on first went leisurely to second, well aware that the Summerville catcher would not dare to throw lest the runner on third should score. With one strike against him and three balls, the man at bat struck

at a rather deceptive drop and started for first. The ball
shot straight at Warner, hot off the bat. The pitcher
found it, but fumbled. Regaining it quickly, he threw to
the home plate, and the Vulcan captain speedily retraced his steps to third. But the batsman was safe at
first, and so the three bases were full.

"Home run! Home run, O'Brien!" shrieked the throng
as the next man, a red-haired little youth, gripped his
stick firmly. O'Brien was quite evidently a favorite as
well as a good player. Warner and Oliver, Summerville's
catcher, met and held a whispered consultation to the
accompaniment of loud ridicule from the audience.
Then the battery took their places.

"Play for the man on third," cried Bob at first base.

Warner's first delivery was a wide throw that almost
passed the catcher. "Ball!" droned the umpire. The men
on bases were playing far off, and intense excitement
reigned. On the next delivery Warner steadied himself
and got a strike over the plate. A shout of applause from
the plucky Summerville spectators shattered the silence. Another strike; again the applause. O'Brien gripped his bat anew and looked surprised and a little
uneasy.

"He can't do it again, O'Brien!" shrieked an excited
admirer in the grand stand.

But O'Brien didn't wait to see. He found the next
delivery and sent it whizzing, a red-hot liner, toward
second. Pandemonium broke loose. Sleeper, Summerville's second baseman, ran forward and got the ball
head-high, glanced quickly aside, saw the runner from

first speeding by, lunged forward, tagged him, and then threw fiercely, desperately home. The sphere shot like a cannon-ball into Oliver's outstretched hands, there was a cloud of yellow dust as Stevens slid for the home plate, and then the umpire's voice droned: "Out, here!"

Summerville, grinning to a man, trotted in, and the little handful of supporters yelled themselves hoarse and danced ecstatically about. Even the Vulcan enthusiasts must applaud the play, though a bit grudgingly. For the first time in many innings, Marty, squatting beside the bats, drew a big sprawling 0 in the tally which he was keeping on the ground, with the aid of a splinter.

It was the last of the eighth inning, and Bob Ayer's turn at the bat. Marty found his especial stick, and uttered an incantation beneath his breath as he held it out.

"We're going to win, Bob," he whispered.

Bob took the bat, shaking his head.

"I'm afraid you don't work as a mascot to-day, Marty," he answered smilingly. But Marty noticed that there was a look of resolution in the captain's face as he walked toward the box, and took heart.

Summerville's admirers greeted Bob's appearance with a burst of applause, and Vulcan's captain motioned the field to play farther out. Vulcan's pitcher tossed his arms above his head, lifted his right foot into the air, and shot the ball forward. There was a sharp *crack*, and the sphere was sailing straight and low toward center field. Bob touched first and sped on to second. Center field and left field, each intent upon the ball, discovered each other's presence only when they were a scant four yards apart. Both paused—and the ball fell to earth! Bob, watching, flew toward third. It was a close shave, but he reached it ahead of the ball in a cloud of dust, and, rising, shook himself in the manner of a dog after a bath. Summerville's supporters were again on their feet, and their shouts were extraordinary in volume, considering their numbers. Vulcan's citizens, after a first burst of anger and dismay, had fallen into chilling silence. Marty hugged himself, and nervously picked out Howe's bat.

The latter, Summerville's short-stop and a mere boy of seventeen, was only an ordinary batsman, and Marty looked to see him strike out. But instead, after waiting with admirable nerve while ball after ball shot by him, he tossed aside his stick and trotted to first base on balls, amid the howls of the visitors. Summerville's first run for four innings was scored a moment later when Bob stole home on a passed ball.

Summerville's star seemed once more in the ascendant. Howe was now sitting contentedly on second base. "Herb" Webster gripped his bat firmly and faced the pitcher. The latter, for the first time during the game, was rattled. Bob, standing back of third, coached Howe with an incessant roar:

"On your toes! Get off! Get off! Come on, now! Come on! He won't throw! Come on, come on! That's right! That's the way! *Now! Wh-o-o-a!* Easy! Look out! Try it again, now!"

Baker received the ball back from second, and again faced the batsman. But he was worried, and proved it by his first delivery. The ball went far to the right of the catcher, and Howe reached third base without hurrying. When Baker again had the ball, he scowled angrily, made a feint of throwing to third, and, turning rapidly, pitched. The ball was a swift one and wild, and Webster drew back, then ducked. The next instant he was lying on the ground, and a cry of dismay arose. The sphere had hit him just under the ear. He lay there unconscious, his left hand still clutching his bat, his face white under its coat of tan. Willing hands quickly lifted him into the dressing-room, and a doctor hurried from the grand stand. Bob, who had helped carry him off the field, came out after a few minutes and went to the bench.

"He's all right now," he announced. "That is, he's not dangerously hurt, you know. But he won't be able to play again to-day. Doctor says he'd better go to the hotel, and we've sent for a carriage. I wish to goodness I knew where to find a fellow to take his place! Think of our coming here without a blessed substitute to our name! I wish I had Magee for a minute; if I wouldn't show him a thing or two! Warner, you'd better take poor Webster's place as runner; I'll tell the umpire."

In another moment the game had begun again, Warner having taken the place of the injured left-fielder at first base, and Sleeper having gone to bat. Vulcan's pitcher was pale and his hands shook as he once more began his work; the injury to Webster had totally unnerved him. The immediate result was that Sleeper knocked a two-bagger that brought Howe home, placed

Warner on third and himself on second; and the ultimate result was that five minutes later, when Oliver fouled out to Vulcan's third-baseman, Sleeper and Wolcott had also scored, and the game stood 12 to 9.

Bob Ayer meanwhile had searched unsuccessfully for a player to take the injured Webster's place, and had just concluded to apply to Vulcan's captain for one of his substitutes, when he turned to find Marty at his side.

"Are yer lookin' fer a feller to play left field?"

"Yes," answered Bob, eagerly. "Do you know of any one?"

Marty nodded.

"Who?"

"Me."

Bob stared in surprise, but Marty looked back without flinching. "I can play, Bob; not like you, of course, but pretty well. And, besides, there ain't no one else, is there? Give me a show, will yer?"

Bob's surprise had given place to deep thought. "Why not?" he asked himself. Of course Marty could play ball; what Summerville boy couldn't, to some extent? And, besides, as Marty said, there was no one else. Bob had seen Marty play a little while the nine was practising, and, so far as he knew, Marty was a better player than any of the Summerville boys who had come with the nine and now sat on the grand stand. The other alternative did not appeal to him: his pride revolted at begging a player from the rival club. He turned and strode to the bench, and Marty eagerly watched him conferring with the others. In a moment he turned and nodded.

A ripple of laughter and ironic applause crept over the stands as Marty, attired in his blue shirt and un-shapen trousers, trotted out to his position in left field. The boy heard it, but didn't care. His nerves were tingling with excitement. It was the proudest moment of his short life. He was playing with the Summerville Baseball Club! And deep down in his heart Marty Brown pledged his last breath to the struggle for victory.

Vulcan started in on their last inning with a deter-mination to add more runs to their score. The first man at bat reached first base on a safe hit to mid field. The second, Vulcan's center-fielder and a poor batsman, struck out ingloriously. When the next man strode to the plate, Bob motioned the fielders to spread out. Marty had scarcely run back a half-dozen yards when the sharp sound of ball on bat broke upon the air, and high up against the blue sky soared the little globe, sailing toward left field. Marty's heart was in his mouth, and for the moment he wished himself back by the bench, with no greater duty than the care of the bats. It was one thing to play ball in a vacant lot with boys of his own age, and another to display his powers in a big game, with half a thousand excited persons watching him. At first base the runner was poised ready to leap away as soon as the ball fell into the fielder's hands—or to the ground! The latter possibility brought a haze before Marty's eyes, and for an instant he saw at least a dozen balls coming toward him; he wondered, in a chill of terror, which one was the real one! Then the mist faded, he stepped back and to the right three paces, telling himself doggedly that he *had* to catch it, put up his hands—

A shout of applause arose from the stands, and the ball was darting back over the field to second base. Marty, with a swelling heart, put his hands in his trousers pockets and whistled to prove his indifference to applause.

The batsman was out, but the first runner stood safely on third base. And then, with two men gone, Vulcan set bravely to work and filled the remaining bases. A safe hit meant two more runs added to Vulcan's score. The fielders, in obedience to Bob's command, crept in. The grand stand and the bleachers were noisy with the cheers of the spectators. Warner glanced around from base to base, slowly settled himself into position, and clutched the ball. The noise was deafening, but his nerves were again steady, and he only smiled carelessly at the efforts of the coaches to rattle him. His arms shot up, and a straight delivery sent the sphere waist-high over the plate.

"Strike!" crooned the umpire. Applause from the Summerville deputation was drowned in renewed shouts and gibes from the rest of the audience. Warner received the ball and again, very deliberately, settled his toe into the depression in the trampled earth. Up shot his arms again, again he lunged forward, and again the umpire called:

"Strike two!"

Oliver tossed the ball to Bob and donned his mask.

The batter stooped and rubbed his hands in the dust, and then gripped the stick resolutely. The ball went back to Warner, and he stepped once more into the box. For a moment he studied the batsman deliberately, a proceeding which seemed to worry that youth, since he lifted first one foot and then the other off the ground and waved his bat impatiently.

"Play ball!" shrieked the grand stand.

Warner smiled, rubbed his right hand reflectively upon his thigh, glanced casually about the bases, lifted one spiked shoe from the ground, tossed his arms up, and shot the ball away swiftly. Straight for the batsman's head it went, then settled down, down, and to the left, as though attracted by Oliver's big gloves held a foot above the earth just back of the square of white marble. The man at bat, his eyes glued to the speeding sphere, put his stick far around, and then, with a sudden gasp, whirled it fiercely. There was a thud as the ball settled cozily into Oliver's leather gloves, a roar from the onlookers, and above it all the umpire's fatal:

"Striker—out!"

Marty, watching breathless and wide-eyed from the field, threw a hand-spring and uttered a whoop of joy. The nines changed places, and the last half of the last inning began with the score still 12 to 9 in favor of Vulcan.

"Play carefully, fellows," shouted Vulcan's captain as Hamilton went to bat. "We've got to shut them out."

"If youse can," muttered Marty, seated on the bench between Bob and Wolcott.

It looked as though they could. Bob groaned as Hamilton popped a short fly into second-baseman's hands, and the rest of the fellows echoed the mournful sound.

"Lift it, Will, lift it!" implored Bob as Pickering strode to the plate. And lift it he did. Unfortunately, however, when it descended it went plump into the hands of right field. In the stand half the throng was on its feet. Bob looked hopelessly at Warner as the pitcher selected a bat.

"Cheer up, Bob," said the latter, grinning. "I'm going to crack that ball or know the reason why!"

The Vulcan pitcher was slow and careful. They had taken the wearied Baker out and put in a new twirler. Warner let his first effort pass unnoticed, and looked surprised when the umpire called it a strike. But he received the next one with a hearty welcome, and sent it speeding away for a safe hit, taking first base amid the wild cheers of the little group of blue-and-white-decked watchers. Hamilton hurried across to coach the runner, and Bob stepped to the plate. His contribution was a swift liner that was too hot for the pitcher, one that placed Warner on second and himself on first. Then, with Hamilton and Sleeper both coaching at the top of their lungs, the Vulcan catcher fumbled a ball at which Howe had struck, and the two runners moved up. The restive audience had overflowed on to the field now, and excitement reigned supreme. Another strike was called on Howe, and for a moment Summerville's chances appeared to be hopeless. But a minute later the batter was limping to first, having been struck with the ball, and the pitcher was angrily grinding his heel into the ground.

"Webster at bat!" called the scorer.

"That's you, Marty," said Wolcott. "If you never do another thing, my boy, *swat that ball!*"

Marty picked out a bat and strode courageously to the plate. A roar of laughter greeted his appearance.

"Get on to Blue Jeans!" "Give us a home run, kid!" "Say, now, sonny, don't fall over your pants!"

It needed just that ridicule to dispel Marty's nervousness. He was angry. How could he help his "pants" being long? he asked himself, indignantly. He'd show those dudes that "pants" hadn't anything to do with hitting a baseball! He shut his teeth hard, gripped the bat tightly, and faced the pitcher. The latter smiled at his adversary, but was not willing to take any chances, with the bases full. And so, heedless of the requests to "Toss him an easy one, Joe!" he delivered a swift, straight drop over the plate.

"Strike!" droned the little umpire, skipping aside.

Marty frowned, but gave no other sign of the chill of disappointment that traveled down his spine. On the bench Wolcott turned to his next neighbor and said, as he shook his head sorrowfully:

"Hard luck! If it had only been some one else's turn now, we might have scored. I guess little Marty's not up to curves."

Marty watched the next delivery carefully—and let it pass.

"Ball!" called the umpire.

Again he held himself in, although it was all he could do to keep from swinging at the dirty-white globe as it sped by him.

"Two balls!"

"That's right, Marty; wait for a good one," called Wolcott, hoping against hope that Marty might get to first on balls. Marty made no answer, but stood there, pale of face but cool, while the ball sped around the bases and at last went back to the pitcher. Again the sphere sped forward. Now was his time! With all his strength he swung his bat—and twirled around on his heel! A roar of laughter swept across the diamond.

"Strike two!" called the umpire.

But Marty, surprised at his failure, yet undaunted, heard nothing save the umpire's unmoved voice. Forward flew the ball again, this time unmistakably wide of the plate, and the little man in the snuff-colored alpaca coat motioned to the right.

"Three balls!"

Bob, restlessly lifting his feet to be off and away on his dash to third, waited with despairing heart. Victory or defeat depended upon the next pitch. A three-bagger would tie the score, a safe hit would bring Sleeper to the bat! But as he looked at the pale-faced, odd-looking figure beside the plate he realized how hopeless it all was. The pitcher, thinking much the same thoughts, prepared for his last effort. Plainly the queer little ragamuffin was no batsman, and a straight ball over the plate would bring the agony to an end. Up went his hand, and straight and sure sped the globe.

Now, there was one kind of ball that Marty knew all

about, and that was a nice, clean, straight one, guiltless of curve or drop or rise, the kind that "Whitey" Peters pitched in the vacant lot back of Keller's Livery Stable. And Marty knew that kind when he saw it coming. Fair and square he caught it, just where he wanted it on the bat. All his strength, heart, and soul were behind that swing. There was a sharp *crack,* a sudden mighty roar from the watchers, and Marty was speeding toward first base.

High and far sped the ball. Center and left fielder turned as one man and raced up the field. Obeying instructions, they had been playing well in, and now they were to rue it. The roar of the crowd grew in volume. Warner, Bob, and Howe were already racing home, and Marty, running as hard as his legs would carry him, was touching second. Far up the field the ball was coming to earth slowly, gently, yet far too quickly for the fielders.

"A home run!" shrieked Wolcott. *"Come on—oh, come on, Marty, my boy!"*

Warner was home, now Bob, and then Howe was crossing the plate, and Marty was leaving second behind him. Would the fielder catch it! He dared look no longer, but sped onward. Then a new note crept into the shouts of the Vulcans, a note of disappointment, of despair. Up the field the center-fielder had tipped the ball with one outstretched hand, but had failed to catch it! At last, however, it was speeding home toward second base.

"Come on! Come on, Marty!" shrieked Bob.

The boy's twinkling feet spurned the third bag and he

swung homeward. The ball was settling into the second-baseman's hands. The latter turned quickly and threw it straight, swift, unswerving toward the plate.

"*Slide!*" yelled Bob and Warner, in a breath.

Marty threw himself desperately forward; there was a cloud of brown dust at the plate, a *thug* as the ball met the catcher's gloves. The little man in the alpaca coat turned away with a grin, and picked up his mask again.

"*Safe, here!*"

The score was 13 to 12 in Summerville's favor; Marty's home run had saved the day!

In another minute or two it was all over. Sleeper had popped a high fly into the hands of the discomfited center-fielder, and the crowds swarmed inward over the diamond.

It was a tired, hungry, but joyous little group that journeyed back to Summerville through the soft, mellow summer twilight. Marty and the leather bat-case occupied a whole seat to themselves. Marty's freckled face was beaming with happiness and pride, his heart sang a pæan of triumph in time to the *clickety-click* of the car-wheels, and in one hand, tightly clenched, nestled a ten-dollar gold piece.

It was his share of the hundred-dollar purse the nine had won, Bob had explained, and it had been voted to him unanimously. And next spring he was to join the team as substitute! And Marty, doubting the trustiness of his pockets, held the shining prize firmly in his fist and grinned happily over the praise and thanks of his companions.

"It wasn't nothin', that home run; any feller could have done that!" And, besides, he explained, he had known all along that they were going to win. "Why,—don't you see?—the other fellers didn't have any mascot!"

Hit or Error?

William Heyliger

No one would ever have picked Buck Everts to blossom forth as an inspiration. Not that there was anything wrong about him, but he had built up a national reputation as a tough nut, a baiter of umpires, a snarling wrangler when close decisions went against him. You remember Buck, of course. Third baseman for the Panthers when the fast-stepping team won three pennants in a row, and rated by the critics as the greatest man who had ever played the hot corner.

After the third pennant Buck was caught in a street car accident, and his right arm was broken in two places. That finished him with baseball. He could still handle anything that came at him, high, low or on the side, but his throwing arm was gone. A third baseman has a long peg to first, and he must let the ball go on a line. With a fast man streaking it down to first, the throw must be just a white streak. Buck, with that smashed arm, couldn't do it.

He dropped out of baseball and came to Woodbury to take charge of the lumber yard of the Woodbury Coal & Lumber Company, which was owned by old John Everts, a second or third cousin. The Everts home stood next to the home of Horace Hicks, the man who was owner, publisher and editor of the *Woodbury Herald*. Old John took Buck in to live with him—and that's where Jimmy Hicks comes into the story.

Jimmy was 16. Thrown on his own resources, circumstances might have toughened him and tuned him to a fighting pitch. He had found life too easy and had grown soft. His pathway had been smoothed, and it came to pass that, in time, he instinctively chose the road of least resistance. His rangy build suggested athletic possibilities; he liked baseball, but for two years at Cromwell Academy he had avoided the fight for place on the school nine. He had musical ability, but had never bothered to cultivate it. He had opinions, but never expressed them. Confronted with a contrary viewpoint, he smiled pleasantly and politely yielded. A disdainful Cromwell boy had once called him a jellyfish. This was not strictly true. It would have been more to the point to have dubbed him a sloth who had never developed a backbone.

The day that ended his sophomore year at Cromwell he came back to Woodbury, and the next morning walked down to the office of the *Herald*. The editorial room had an early-morning air of desertion. His father, in a little walled-off space, was running his eyes through a stack of out-of-town newspapers. Two men were wading through the overnight copy. The reporters had not yet begun to straggle in from their districts, and all the desks in the center of the room were empty and idle. The door leading to the composing room opened, and the sport editor came through carrying a sheaf of damp galley proofs.

"Hello, Jimmy," he greeted. "Back from school, eh? Remember the time last summer you said Buck Everts was the greatest third baseman in the game? Well, you can tell him all about it now; he's your next door neighbor."

"Buck?"

"Buck himself. I'm running the story this afternoon. Funny none of us ever knew that John Everts is his cousin. He's come to Woodbury to work in the lumber yard, and he's living right next to you. His baseball days are over, but he certainly was a bear-cat in his time. Look him up; he's worth knowing."

Jimmy, for all his polite aloofness, had found time to worship at the shrine of two heroes. One of these was Buck; the other was Arlie Pierce, star pitcher of the Cromwell nine. His worship of Buck had been open; his veneration of Arlie had been secret. Arlie was the campus idol. The biggest fellows in the school flocked in his wake. Jimmy, not used to going out for what he wanted, could not even go out for friendship. He hung on the edge of a crowd of worshippers, a mere shadow, reluctant to push forward and claim his share of attention. At the end of two years Arlie scarcely knew his name.

With Buck things had been different. The Panthers'

third baseman had the vague, legendary quality of one who lives far away. Jimmy could speak of him with freedom, as he might speak of the King of Siam, and never expect to meet him. But now Buck was here, and the same shrinking that had held him aloof from Arlie began to work its spell on him again.

At noon, from the safe retreat of his porch, he watched Buck come home to eat—a short, rugged man who cocked his cap to one side and walked with a swagger that was well known to the fans in the big league cities. He saw the man go back to work, and his heart fluttered. An urge that he could not explain sent him that afternoon toward the village field with bat, ball and glove. Hours later he came back, with the whistle of the paper mill across the river booming its hoarse notice of quitting time. He dropped on the grass of the lawn, the bat across his knees, and was there when Buck Everts came swaggering up the street.

The big leaguer, almost at the Everts' porch, saw him, hesitated and then came striding across the grass.

"You the fellow who thinks I was the greatest third baseman in the game?" Buck's grin was wide and friendly. "The sport ed was telling me about you. Well, I guess I was as good as any of them, if I do say it myself. Play baseball?"

"A—a little." Jimmy's stammer was a confession of his confusion. To hold conversation with the great Buck had never entered the wildest of his dreams.

"What position?"

Hit or Error?

"I like to play third."

"Now you're talking. What's that school you go to the sport ed was telling me about?"

"Cromwell."

"That's it. Did you make the nine?"

"No, sir."

"Huh! Somebody beat you out of it?" Buck reached down for the bat. "Use this? Too light. Get one about two ounces heavier. Get down there and let me hit you a few. Maybe they won't beat you out for it next year."

Jimmy scrambled to his feet, caught up his glove, and walked down the lawn. It was plain to be seen that Buck thought he had turned out for the nine, but had lost the position to another man. The boy flushed, and could not understand why the blood should mount to his cheeks. However, even in the intoxication of the moment, he knew that he would not tell Buck the truth because it would rob him of something Buck thought he had.

The man swung the ball upward and moved the bat forward to meet it. To Jimmy's eyes the sphere seemed to skim the grass with bewildering speed. He made a frenzied stab with his bare hand—and missed. Ten minutes later Buck tossed the bat aside.

"That's all for now. I know why you lost out, kid. You haven't got a thing when the ball's hit to your right. Your start is slow. You've got lead in your feet and glue in your arms. You've got no knack of getting them on your right side a-tall. Want to make the nine next year?"

"Yes," Jimmy said very suddenly.

"All right. To-morrow you hit to me and I'll show you

how it's done. After that you get about half-an-hour chasing grounders every night. You leave it to me, kid, and you'll play third for Cromwell. See you tomorrow."

"I—I'm not much of a hitter," said Jimmy.

"Leave it to me," said Buck. "I've peeled the curtains away from more than one batting eye."

And so, for the first time in his life, Jimmy Hicks found that he wanted something badly enough to make a fight for it. Day after day Buck slashed the ball at him, and day after day he ran himself ragged to an accompaniment of barking, rasping directions. Before and after the practice Buck was the soul of genial companionship; while the work was on he was a merciless driver. Had Jimmy kept track of the hits he would have known that most of them were on his right side, but he was too much concerned with getting the ball at all to bother his head with keeping track of where it went.

"Kid," said Buck, "you've got a bum pair of hands."

Jimmy surveyed his palms and fingers. "What's the matter with them!"

"Oh, I don't mean it that way. It's a form of speaking we have in the leagues. When we find a baby who's got a knack of getting his paws on the ball and holding it, we say he's got a good pair of hands."

"Then—then I won't make it, will I?"

"Who says so?" Buck bristled. "Ain't I showing you how? You're not much of a natural fielder, but you can do a pretty good mechanical job."

"I'd like to make it," Jimmy said after a while. "There's a fellow at school—"

"Think you'd make a hit with him by getting into the batting order?"

Jimmy nodded.

"Leave it to me," said Buck. "What's this guy's name?"

"Arlie Pierce."

"Well, you and Arlie are as good as pals."

That was the joyous prospect that Jimmy, six weeks later, took back with him to Cromwell.

Luck seemed to be with him. Comfortably settled in his dormitory room, he learned that Rice, last year's third baseman, was not coming back to school. The same day, leaving the school office, he came face to face with Arlie.

"Hello!" The pitcher gave him a glance in which doubt was mingled with perplexity. "Your name's Hicks, isn't it? I thought so. You look more rugged than you did. What were you doing all summer?"

"Playing ball. I'm coming out for the nine. Third base."

"We'll have to find a new man for third," Arlie said thoughtfully. "What team did you play with?"

"Oh, I didn't play with a team, but Buck Everts coached me."

The pitcher's eyes opened. "Not—"

"Yes," Jimmy said with inward satisfaction; "the Panthers' old third baseman."

Arlie swung him around by the shoulders and pushed him toward the dormitory building. "Come up to my room," he said, "and tell me all about him. Where does he live since he quit the big show?"

"He lives next door to me."

"He does?" The pitcher urged him forward with a hand on his arm. "Hurry. I want to hear it all before supper."

And thus was the seed of friendship sown between Arlie Pierce and Jimmy Hicks.

That first visit was followed by many others. The two boys occupied separate rooms on the same floor, and by and by they formed the habit of dropping in on each other, loaded down with books, for an evening of study. From the shadowy obscurity of being a mere student, one of the hundreds of unhonored and unsung, Jimmy found himself transported to the realms of the mighty. He had trod the earth with a great man, and became a mirror of reflected glory. The whole school heard of his contact with Buck, and eagerly snapped up the crumbs of anecdote that fell from his lips. He had come back to Cromwell hoping that Arlie would admit him to the magic of an inner circle. Instead, by a trick of fate he found himself on equal terms with the school hero.

Yet he never quite lost a certain feeling of inferiority where Arlie was concerned. It was as though, deep within him, he feared that the miracle of the pitcher's friendship would not last. The diffident streak in him began to come to the surface. Bit by bit, as the fall and winter wore on, he fell into the old habit of shifting ground, surrendering opinions and smiling his smile of conciliation.

Hit or Error?

"Great Scott," Arlie cried in exasperation one night, "you don't have to swallow everything I say. Haven't you got any ideas of your own?"

Jimmy flushed a bit. "Can't a fellow be agreeable?"

"Apple sauce!" Arlie said in disgust. "Isn't there anything you'll say and stick to?"

"Yes. I'm going to play third base."

The pitcher stared at him a moment, started to say something, and stopped. Jimmy had the uncomfortable conviction that Arlie had an idea that he might not make it.

Next day there was nothing to denote that their friendship had passed through a flurry of rough water. But in the back of Jimmy's mind lurked the fear that, come spring, he might lose out. Common sense began to point out considerations that he had ignored. He had acquired skill in fielding a ball, but he had had practically no work in throwing to bases, in judging what to do on a fielder's choice, or in dovetailing his movements with those of other men—the thing that is called teamwork. Then, too, there was Dixie Orth. Dixie had tried for third last year, but Rice had beaten him out. Dixie would try again this year. Dixie had the advantage of experience.

Many a man, finding his courage beginning to shake, has sought to talk himself back to confidence. Jimmy tried the same trick. The campus expected him, because of his summer as Buck's pupil, to make the nine. He began to talk as though his selection were as good as accomplished. One February night, with Arlie's room comfortably filled, he steered the same channel—the things that Buck had taught him and Buck's prediction that he would surely win out. It was not until he had finished that he noticed that Dixie was standing over near the door.

"You shouldn't have gassed that way," Arlie said when the crowd was gone. "You'll have to cut it out."

"I didn't know Dixie was there," Jimmy defended.

"Of course you didn't. I don't mean that. But if I were you I'd stop speaking about Buck and about what Buck promised you."

"Why?"

"It might prove embarrassing. You know the athletic committee has been looking for a baseball coach. Well, I guess they've found him. I heard just after supper that they had sent a contract to Buck."

The Panthers' old third baseman arrived at Cromwell early in March, his derby hat pulled down a bit above his right eye and his walk a confident, cocky swagger. The school held a meeting in the gym that night and worked up a lot of enthusiasm. Speeches were made by a faculty advisor, by the chairman of the athletic committee, and by Bagby, the captain of the nine. Then a great shout went up for "Coach, coach, coach."

Buck, to whom baseball had been a bread-and-butter business, gave the shortest talk of the night.

"Lots of pep," he said dryly, "but games ain't won from the grandstand. Now let's get out and play some ball. We start to-morrow, right here, at 4 o'clock."

At 4 o'clock Jimmy was there. He had met Buck
shortly after his arrival, had shaken hands with him,
and then had effaced himself from the picture. From the
time that Arlie had told him who the coach was to be, he
had decided upon this course. If he had not spoken so
freely of Buck, if he had not boasted so loudly of his own
sureness of success, things might have been different.
As it was he had sense enough to know that he would
have to guard against campus gossip, and give nobody a
chance to say that he was too close to the coach. His
plan of self-abnegation gave him a feeling of merited
virtue.

At the gym he gave his name and his history. He had
no real experience playing third. No; he had not tried for
the nine last year. He caught a flash of surprise in Buck's
eyes.

Then Dixie followed him with his two years on a
grammar school team and his year as a substitute at
Cromwell. Jimmy bit his lips.

"What wins ball games," Buck told the candidates,
"is speed. From to-day we're building for a team that
will have the sparkle. Cap. Bagby, here, will divide you
up—half to the handball court, half to the gym track.
When the whistle blows you reverse. Got that? Don't try
to commit suicide in a day. You've got about thirty
afternoons before you get outdoors. Take it easy."

Jimmy was counted into the tracks squad. Three
times around the track and air seemed to be the scarcest
commodity in the world. He slowed to a walk.

"That's right, kid," came Buck's voice. "No need of

trying to kill yourself. Walk about a hundred steps and then trot."

Jimmy walked—and Dixie, breathing easily, passed him like a flitting shadow.

For a week his legs, his back, his arms, ached with a wrenching soreness. More than once he was tempted to quit, the old spirit of surrender whispering to him to get out and take his comfort. Had he not spoken so confidently of his prospects, he would probably have swung up that old road of least resistance. Now pride, the fear of ridicule, held him to his task in spite of outward soreness and inner squirmings. Had he only known it, it was the first time in his life he had really won a victory over himself. For, compared to this, last summer's practice with Buck had been child's play.

In all that first week Buck did not speak to him three times; and though he had agreed with himself on a policy of keeping in the background, the coach's attitude piqued him.

"You'd imagine," he complained to Arlie, "that he had never seen me before."

The pitcher looked at him curiously. "You're not looking for favors, are you?"

Jimmy awoke to his mistake and achieved a sickly smile. "I was only fooling," he said. Arlie frowned impatiently. Afterwards Jimmy asked himself bitterly why he had not told the truth—that he had not expected Buck in view of past events to treat him so completely as just one of the squad.

And then came a day when the soreness was gone.

His muscles responded like oiled springs. Buck brought out baseballs, and the candidates ranged across the gym and began to throw them around. The pitchers and the catchers retired to the track.

"Just to break in the throwing muscles and get your hands used to the feel of the ball," said Buck. "The first fellow who tries any fancy stuff gets the gate."

The squad obeyed, having already learned that the cocky Buck, while short on words and the niceties of grammar, was long on discipline. Jimmy, watching Dixie, decided that there was nothing outstanding about his rival's play. Dixie took the ball with a negligent flip of his glove and threw it with a lazy movement of his arm. He seemed to be a careless, happy-go-lucky youth who took baseball as a sort of joke.

But once the squad got outdoors and pranced across the turf of Cromwell Field, Dixie's spirit was reborn. There had been a race for places, and he had cornered third. He kicked the bag, straightened it with his toe, spat in his glove and shook a fist at Buck, who was waiting at the plate to hit.

"Come on, old timer," he yelled. "Hit one down here with some big league stuff behind it."

Buck sent a smoking grounder almost along the foul line. Dixie made a stab, and the ball struck his glove and rolled away. Headlong he dove for it and, from one knee, threw fast and true to first.

"Not so rotten," said Buck, and hammered the ball at the second baseman.

At the end of the afternoon Jimmy walked back slowly to the gym. His throws to first had been uncertain. Four times the ball had been hit to his right—twice to go bounding past him and once to be fumbled. And in front of them all Buck had called: "Same old weakness, kid. Hop to it with more speed."

He survived the first cut, and the second. He was trying now with a desperate effort; but the plays that he made only by giving every last ounce of himself, Dixie seemed to make with ease. One day, on the bench, Arlie suddenly put a hand on his shoulder.

"You're certainly fighting for it," he said in a whisper. "Good luck."

A warmth, such as he had never known before, ran through his veins. Then and there was born the thought of him and Arlie rooming together next year. It grew on him. That night he mentioned it to Arlie.

The pitcher grinned. "That wouldn't be half bad, would it?" Jimmy took it as a tacit acceptance.

Three days before the first game the squad was cut for the last time, and Jimmy found himself out. His eyes sought Arlie's as Buck called his name, but Arlie was apparently absorbed in examining a bruised finger. In twos and threes the discards walked back to the gym, and presently, alone, he followed them, confronted with the melancholy necessity of clearing out his locker.

"Wait a minute, kid," came Buck's voice. Jimmy waited, and they fell into step. The boy's face was black—his thoughts were blacker. Oh, the coach would talk to him now. He had been cast aside. He wasn't wanted.

"Kid," Buck said feelingly, "you certainly threw some high and fast ones before I came down. In I walk, and find you swinging some wicked conversation about how good you were and how I said you'd make the nine. Fine for me, wasn't it? Half the school was watching to see how I'd handle you. Mind, I'm not panning you. You couldn't guess that they were going to offer me a job here. If you'd had the stuff I'd have stuck you in. I'm after a winner, and the best player is the chocolate drop with me. I'm trying to fix it so that you can stick around. Wear a uniform and all that. What killed you off this year was lack of experience. Next year you ought to be all set for glory. Do you know how to boxscore a game?"

"Yes; I've done it for my father's paper."

"All right: here's the play. I name you official scorer. You keep your locker. You wear a uniform. Afternoons you get some of the practice. On the bench, during a game, you use your eyes and your head. Watch how things are done and then, during next day's practice, try to do them a little better. I want to hold you with this baseball crowd. I've got a two-year contract, and next year I'm figuring you're going to be ripe. How about it?"

"You said I'd make the nine this year."

"Kid," Buck said frankly, "I did the craziest thing a man can do. I called you safe without seeing the play. I didn't know this outfit. I thought it was just a kid team. Well, I've made you the offer. Take it or leave it."

"I'll take it," said Jimmy.

He took the berth, not because he thought it an honor but because it held him in the squad and kept him closer to Arlie. After Buck had left him, he retraced his steps and came back to the diamond. Dixie, standing on the third base bag, spoke to him as he passed, but he did not answer. Arlie, sitting on the bench, was looking his way, and seemed to be frowning. He waved a summons, and the pitcher came out to meet him, a strange look of gravity on his face.

Jimmy told of Buck's offer. There was something quiet—too quiet—in the way Arlie accepted the news. A sudden fear grabbed at Jimmy's heart.

"It's all right about next year, Arlie—rooming together—isn't it?"

"We don't have to decide that until June, do we?" the pitcher asked. Then Buck called him, and he walked out toward the hurling mount. With a sinking heart Jimmy decided that Arlie was cutting away from him because he had not made the nine. Before the day was out he had to revise this judgment, for that night Arlie came to his room to study, and was as friendly and companionable as he had been before. After the pitcher had gone, long after he himself should have been in bed, Jimmy sat at a window, in the dark, and tried to puzzle things out. What had he done that Arlie should view him as no longer desirable? And if he was not desirable, why should Arlie continue to bother with him at all? Something mysterious and obscure had come between them. What it was he did not know, but he did know this—that he would not give up hope until he and Arlie went home in June. The fighting spirit was growing upon him.

The day of the first game Buck presented him with a new scorebook.

"Kid," said the coach, "make no mistake, you've got a man's-size job. Every fielding average rests on your judgment. Even the number of hits a pitcher allows depends on how you score them. Hits or errors? You're the baby who has the say-so. A lot of people think you can throw a scorebook at anybody. That's a laugh. You might as well say you can let players slide into bases, feet first and all stiffened out, and break their legs. A bird who doesn't know what's what can do some goofy scoring and get a good team scrapping among themselves. The better the player, the more anxious he is to have the record straight. Get that, kid?

Jimmy nodded.

"Hop to it. You're the boss. Whatever you put down in that book goes."

Jimmy scored that game with more seriousness than he had ever brought to a similar undertaking for the sport editor of the Woodbury *Herald*. Only in a secondary way did he pay attention to the score. He knew that Arlie was pitching good ball and that Cromwell was winning. He knew it in the same sort of unconscious way that he appreciated the warmth of the April sun on his knees. Practically his entire attention was given to watching the ball.

In the seventh inning, with Captain Bagby on second, his fountain pen slipped from his fingers and rolled behind his feet. As he stooped to recover it, his eyes off the field, a sudden cry from the crowd told him that something out of the ordinary had happened. His hand felt for the pen; his eyes sought the field. Bagby had been caught napping off second, and was prancing between second and third in an attempt to avoid being run down and tagged. Enemy players were closing in on him. The pen kept eluding Jimmy's hand and he had to look for it. When he raised his eyes again Bagby, brushing the dust from his uniform, was walking back toward the bench, and the enemy players were jubilantly scurrying back to their positions.

"I saw the players who were in the run-up," said Jimmy, "but I missed the finish. Who made the putout?"

"Catcher," said Dixie. "He got Bagby sliding into third."

Jimmy ignored the third baseman and looked at Arlie. "Who gets the putout? Catcher?"

"Didn't Dixie tell you?" Arlie asked sharply.

Jimmy flushed, and bent down over the scorebook to mark the play. Ever since his failure to make the nine, a soreness had been growing in him against Dixie. He had adopted a childish attitude of silent scorn, as though by this means he might wither the other boy's victory. That Dixie had done him no wrong had had no effect upon his resentment. Up to the time Arlie had rebuked him, he had taken a grim pleasure in snubbing the player who had beaten him out. Now, all at once, he was conscious that he had acted like a fool.

A Cromwell boy popped to the shortstop for the second out, and Dixie walked up to the plate. Jimmy slid along the bench to Arlie.

"I shouldn't have done that," he said in an undertone. "It won't hppen again."

Arlie smiled. "I thought you weren't that kind of loser."

"I didn't think of it that way until you spoke—"

Arlie shook his head in a way that bespoke despair and exasperation. "Jimmy," he said, "why is it somebody always has to make you see things? Why don't you get some firsthand viewpoints?" Dixie hit to the box and was thrown out, and Arlie strode away from the bench to pitch the beginning of the eighth.

Jimmy knew that he had disappointed Arlie again— that the room-mate idea had been thrust just a little farther away. He resolved to win back to a friendly footing with Dixie, not because of the effect it might have on Arlie, but because it was the only decent thing to do.

And yet he found it hard to make friendly advances, or even to speak with casual ease. A shy reticence paralyzed his tongue, strangled his vocal cords, and stopped his lips. And so, so far as Dixie was concerned, he sat mute upon the bench—and Arlie watched him with frowning, misunderstanding eyes.

The season ran on. Game followed game. Sometimes Cromwell won, sometimes she lost. Jimmy found himself writing the baseball page for the school magazine, and contributing stories of Cromwell's games to the local newspaper at $2 a column. Even though he had not made the nine this gave him standing, and the crowd continued to drop in on him after supper in the school dining-hall. If, in those days, he now and then looked at Arlie with an unspoken appeal, the pitcher pretended not to see it. And so came, at last, the big game of the year against Brockton.

That morning Jimmy received a note from an old friend, the sport editor of his father's paper.

"Good luck, but prepare for the worst. I've checked up on a dozen sport pages and the opinion is that Cromwell will lose. Brockton carries six murderous hitters in its lineup."

Jimmy, thinking this might be news to Buck, took the letter to the coach.

"Shown this to anybody?" Buck demanded.

"No."

"Good!" The coach struck a match and burned the letter. "Told anybody about it?"

"No."

"Wise kid. If you do I'll chase you out of town with a bat. Baseball is like a lot of other things in life—a closed mouth bites into no trouble."

Jimmy took away from the interview the conviction that the truth was in the newspaper reports, and that Buck knew it. Heretofore, he had been a scoring machine, marking the plays with cold-blooded precision. That afternoon with 2,000 rooters singing, and cheering, and stamping in the stands, the importance of the contest worked its spell upon him and his heart did queer things in his breast. The hand that had been steady all season trembled as it wrote the batting orders.

It was Arlie's game. Tall and graceful, the pitcher warmed up in front of the Cromwell stand. By newspaper prediction he was due to-day to fail, to have his curves slaughtered, to be devastated and buried under a withering volley of drives. Jimmy looked at the crowd that would see his friend's downfall, and felt a lump tighten in his throat.

Arlie came back to the bench, ran his pitching arm into sweater, and leaned back at ease waiting for the game to start.

"How was your control out there?" Buck asked.

"I was putting the ball where I wanted it to go."

"That's shooting. No playing around today; pitch to them. Make every shot count. Keep the batters in the hole and you'll be walking on the top of the world."

The Brockton coach came over.

"Got a first-class scorer?" he asked Buck.

"First class."

"O.K., then. his score goes for us, too."

Ten minutes later Arlie was on the mound, the first Brockton boy was at the plate, and the game was on. Buck, his hat pulled down low, chewed on a blade of grass and watched the field through narrowed eyes.

Arlie pitched the first ball.

"Strike one!" ruled the umpire.

The next pitch was hit to Dixie, and the batter was out at first. His teammate fouled out on the first ball. The third boy took a called strike, and then hoisted a fly to the right fielder.

"What did I tell you?" Buck demanded. "You pitched only five balls that inning. Keep the batter in the hole and you'll be sitting pretty."

Bagby walked out to the plate, hitched his trousers, dug his right foot into the dirt, grew tense as the Brockton pitcher wound up—and then drove the first ball into deep center for a home run.

Jimmy found himself on his feet banging his score-book against Dixie's arm and cheering. The nine, in a frenzy of chatter, was calling for more action and half-a-dozen more runs. It looked at that moment as though the final verdict might be written before the game was five minutes old. But the Brockton pitcher was not the type to be broken by one unexpected blow. Slowly and methodically he worked, and three Cromwell batters went out in order. Dixie, the last man to be retired, struck out on three pitched balls and threw the bat from him in disgust.

At the end of the fifth inning the score was still 1 to 0. The stands had cheered themselves out, and had reached a stage of breathless hush. Every moment that one run loomed bigger. The strain was beginning to tell upon the players. Arlie, between the inning halves, sat with his eyes half-closed, the muscles of his mouth twitching.

"Good work," Jimmy whispered in his ear.

He smiled absently, but answered not a word.

An inning later the score was still unchanged. Jimmy

suddenly sat bolt upright as though an electric current had touched his spine.

"Arlie hasn't given them a hit yet," he cried.

In the excitement of the game nobody had noticed this save Buck. The coach favored the score keeper with a murderous glance. He wanted Arlie out there pitching for the game, with no thought in his mind of box-score records.

"That Brockton guy's only given us two hits," he said.

But an inning later the fact was plain, and could no longer be denied. Arlie was on his way to a no-hit game.

"Any other Cromwell pitcher ever do it?" Jimmy asked. "No? Gosh, Arlie, if you can only turn the trick!"

"Only six more men to get," cried Dixie.

"Get 'em," came from Bagby. "Oh, boy! A no-hit game. Wouldn't that look like something in the papers to-morrow. It will go on the sport pages all over the country. Put it over, Arlie, and they'll all know about Cromwell to-morrow."

Buck sighed under his breath: There was no sense in going against such a tide.

"How's the arm?" he asked. "Strong?"

The pitcher nodded.

"Go ahead; shoot for it."

Arlie's face went white. Jimmy's heart missed half-a-dozen beats.

The stand had awakened to how close Cromwell's pitcher was to baseball's Hall of Fame. A cheer greeted him as he went out to pitch the eighth, and grew in

volume as the first batter fouled to Bagby. The next
Brockton boy hit long and far, and an audible groan
turned to a shriek as Cromwell's right fielder raced
under the ball and pulled it down. And the next batter
popped to Arlie himself.

Cromwell's song of triumph burst from the stands.
The cheer leaders did not call for it. It was spontaneous,
impulsive, clarion.

Jimmy sprang from the bench. "Only three more,
Arlie; only three more."

The pitcher was trembling. Sitting next to him,
Jimmy could feel the twitching of his arm, of his leg.
The color that had gone from his face had not come
back. Cromwell hitters went up to the plate and came
back discomfited. Arlie paid no attention. His mind now
was on only one thing.

Bagby shook his shoulder. "Time to do it again. Last
crack. We're with you. They won't get a ball past us."

"Feed them that drop," Dixie pleaded. "They can't
touch it."

"Easy," said Buck. "Take your time and it's all
yours."

Arlie stood up to shed his sweater. As he stooped to
throw the garment on the bench, his head came close to
Jimmy's.

"Root for me," he said. His voice was hoarse.

The pitcher got off to a bad start, and served two wide
balls to the first batter. The next pitch was over, and the
batter drove a savage liner past Bagby.

Hit or Error?

"Oh!" Jimmy moaned.

But the hit was foul by inches. Then the batter hit weakly to the box, and was thrown out.

Jimmy's spirits soared. "Only two more, Arlie," he cried. His voice was drowned in the bedlam of the stands. The cheering had lost all order, all rhythm. It had become a frenzy of hope and expectation.

Arlie was wiping his hands on his uniform as though they were sweating. A Brockton boy, crouched at the plate, moved a nervous bat and waited. The pitcher delivered the ball.

The stands roared as wood met leather. The grounder went straight toward the second baseman. He dug it from the dirt, set himself, and threw the runner out.

"Only one more!" It was Jimmy's voice, lifted in a shriek.

The roaring of the stands was as the roaring of the sea. After the out, the infielders threw the ball around. Arlie walked halfway toward his catcher and then walked back to the mound.

"Can't stand still," Buck muttered. "Keyed up too high."

Bagby threw the pitcher the ball. The cheering tapered off and died. A quiet, startling in its contrast to the tumult, settled over the field. Arlie, the ball against his breast, waited for his catcher's sign.

Buck was muttering again. "Kid, pitch right to him. You're too nervous to try the corners. It's your only chance."

Arlie seemed to have come to the same conclusion. One moment, stretched far back, he was poised; the next, the ball shot forward. The batter swung.

Crack!

"Right on the nose," Buck sighed. He knew the sound. Something like a united sob came from the stands. The scorebook fell from Jimmy's hands.

The ball, on a line, had shot toward third. Afterwards there were those who said it went so fast they did not see it. Dixie made a desperate sidelong plunge. The ball struck the frantic, outstretched fingers of his glove and then carromed off his hands and rolled into left field. The batter raced all the way to second.

Half the stands were crying, "It's a hit;" the other half were shouting, "It's an error." Jimmy's eyes were blinded with a stinging mist. He rubbed the tears from his eyes, reached down for the scorebook, and stole a glance out at the field. Arlie stood there motionless now, looking over at the bench.

"It's an error," Jimmy said fiercely, and poised his pen to charge not a hit to the credit of the batter but an error to the discredit of Dixie.

But something stopped the pen. He knew the rule observed by scorers everywhere—a ball, batted too hard to be handled cleanly, had to be charged as a hit, even though a fielder managed to get his hands upon it.

But after all, it was entirely a matter of the score-keeper's judgment. If he believed that Dixie should have held the ball, or at least have knocked it down and have thrown the runner out at first, then the third baseman should be charged with an error and Arlie given credit for a no-hit game. Just one little mark in the book and Arlie would have his honor.

"It's an error," Jimmy told himself again.

But still the pen did not move to write it so. The stands were still in turmoil.

"Arlie'd never forgive me," Jimmy told himself miserably.

"Root for me," the pitcher had pleaded. Hit or error? The pen shook in Jimmy's grasp. So easy to mark it as his longings dictated, and yet— He had been trusted. Buck had told him that he held the records in his hands. But an error meant so little to Dixie, and a no-hit game meant so much to Arlie. He had asked Arlie to be his roommate. Perhaps, if he gave the pitcher the benefit of the doubt— But the scoring rules laid down the law that, in case of doubt, the batter was always to be credited with a hit.

"They—they trusted me to do it right," Jimmy said in a choking voice.

A yelp from the stands brought his eyes back to the field. The Cromwell nine was running in; the game was over. He heard someone say Arlie had made a quick throw to second and had caught the runner napping off the bag. Then the nine was clamoring around the bench.

"What was it?" Arlie demanded.

"I—" Jimmy wet his lips. "I had to score it as a hit. It was too hard a ball for Dixie to handle."

"Shucks!" Dixie said in disgust; "I was hoping I had

mussed it up for an error."

They did not question his judgment. Jimmy's heart swelled. Yet he was afraid to look at Arlie. Now, at last, he marked the hit, and the out that had followed it and remained bent over the scorebook for a long time. When he looked up the pitcher was on his way to the gym, surrounded by a crowd of admirers who had come tumbling out of the stands.

"Tough on Arlie," said Buck.

"Tough?" Jimmy demanded bitterly. "How tough do you think it was on me?"

"Kid," said the coach who understood, "a square guy always marks 'em as he sees 'em."

Jimmy closed the book and left the bench. For the first time that season he regretted he had worn a uniform; it would have been so much easier to have slipped away to his dormitory room. But he had to change his clothes. He opened the gym door and went in.

The players seemed to have forgotten that they had won the game. They were still talking of how close Arlie had come to what no other Cromwell pitcher had ever accomplished. Every word stabbed him. He noticed that, in all the buzz of talk, Arlie was silent and thoughtful. That stabbed him even harder. He hurried out of his uniform and into his street clothes, and moved toward the door.

"Wait for me, Jimmy," Arlie called.

He waited outside because he could not bear to linger in the dressing room. What Arlie would say to him he did not know. The decision had rested with him—hit or error—and he had decided against his friend. What a fine turn for friendship to take!

Five minutes later Arlie came out. There was a peculiarly dreamy expression on his face.

"You spoke to me about rooming together next year," he said. "Still feel that way? Then let's hustle over to the office and put in a claim for that big corner room on the second floor before somebody beats us to it. That room would be peachy."

Jimmy was bewildered. "You mean you'll room with me after—after—"

"Just for that reason," Arlie said softly. "I was afraid to take a chance on you, Jimmy. If I had to go through a year of studying, living, getting up and going to bed in the same room with a fellow who did nothing but 'yes' me, and agree with me, and salve me, I'd want to murder him. I want a friend I can depend on to stand by me when I'm right and tell me bluntly when I'm wrong. After to-day, Jimmy, I haven't any doubts. You'll mark them as you see them, as Buck would say. You're there. You'll do. Let's hustle and get that room."

The Strikeout King

Franklin M. Reck

It wasn't until after the third game of the season that String Johnson, State College's leading pitcher, had visions of a record. Then suddenly, as he sat before his locker, dressing for practice, it all came to him in a vivid, complete picture.

Seventeen strikeouts in his first two games! If he went on at this rate, he'd challenge the mark of the famous Bull Donnelly, who had struck out an average of nine men per game in his last year at State. Bull was now doing well in the major leagues, taking his regular turn for the Green Sox, and his college record still remained untouched in the Valley Conference.

Now, for the first time, String Johnson saw clearly the glorious possibility of duplicating Bull's career. He had often dreamed of signing a major league contract, of playing ball in the summer and going to law school in the winter, but the dream had always seemed far-away and shadowy. Now it was clear-cut and brilliant, as if someone had yanked up the shade and let in the sunshine.

The vision brought a smile to his lean face, and his spirits bounded. With a swoop he took his glove from the bench and trotted toward the exit leading to the playing field. Two other players were going out the door—Don Maxwell, catcher, and Bob Waddey, right fielder. String slung his long arm around Don Maxwell's shoulder.

"Don!" he yelped. "Grin, my boy! Can't you see the sun is shining?"

Don squinted outside. "So it is," he said. "What eyes you have!"

"The birds are blossoming and the leaves twittering," String chortled. "Let's sing. The flowers that bloom in the spring, tra-la—"

The square-built Waddey scratched his head and looked at String quizzically. "What's the good news?" he asked. "Have you got inside dope that the depression is over?"

"Not yet," String said cheerfully, "but soon."

The three players trotted down the stone steps leading to the ground and stopped. In front of them stood a student, barring the way. He had on a faded brown sweater with frayed sleeves. His corduroy pants just reached the tops of his well-worn tan Oxfords.

"Can you fellows tell me where to report?" he asked.

"Report for what?" String asked.

"Baseball."

"Baseball," String said, putting a long finger to his high forehead. "Good old baseball. Um—the freshman squad?"

"No—the varsity."

Something in the words struck String humorously. Perhaps it was the confident tone in which they were uttered. Or maybe String's own high spirits. Anyhow, he laughed.

"Reporting for the varsity—now?" he asked. "Son— where have you been these many weeks?"

"Working."

"What position do you expect to occupy?"

The student looked at String a moment and then deliberately turned to Waddey. "Can you tell me where to report?" he asked quietly.

"I guess you want to talk to Coach Hendricks," Waddey said, starting for the field. "Come on along."

String and Don Maxwell watched Waddey depart with the corduroyed student.

"Snubbed," Don said grinning. "The great String Johnson, snubbed by what appears to be a sophomore."

String laughed good-humoredly.

"Don," he confided impulsively. "Something tells me this is going to be my big year."

"Bigger than last year?" Don asked. "You lost only one game last year."

"But I needed a lot of horseshoes." String dismissed the previous season with an eloquent gesture. "I feel like a different person this year. Stronger. And that curve—"

"That curve," Don said solemnly, "is one of the hottest I've ever seen.

"It *is* good," String admitted without boasting. "And from now on, whenever we need a third strike, we'll use it."

String and Don walked over beyond the first-base line, but they had barely begun warming up before they heard the coach calling them. They looked toward home plate and saw the coach standing there, with Waddey and the corduroyed student beside him. Wondering what was up, the two trotted over.

Coach Hendricks wore a mackintosh, street trousers, and spikes. His face was sharply cut, and a pair of alert eyes peered out from under the visor of his baseball cap.

"Toss Jarvis, here, a few pitches," he said briefly, indicating the candidate. "Don, you let him have your mitt." He turned to the new candidate. "Go ahead."

String looked at the new man more closely than he had on the gym steps and noted the eager, confident face, the well-set shoulders and straight legs. With a friendly nod, String walked out to the mound and waited while Jarvis took his position behind the plate.

"All set?" String called out amiably.

The catcher nodded, and String tossed over a couple of easy pitches to start things off. Then he grinned a warning at the squatting figure.

"The curve ball," he called.

"Let her come."

String uncorked his curve, and listened for the familiar pistol report, but instead there was only a thud as the ball hit the rim of Jarvis' glove and dropped to the ground at his feet. The catcher straightened up and looked toward the coach.

"The mitt's too big," he said apologetically. "Is there a smaller one? Or a first baseman's mitt?"

A dozen near-by players had gathered to look on, and several of them laughed aloud.

"I'm not kidding," Jarvis said, embarrassed. "A big glove handcuffs me."

The coach looked over toward first base. "Oh, Todd!" he called.

A raw-boned six-footer trotted over.

"Give this boy your mitt."

String looked on in amazement while Jarvis took the thin slice of sponge from Don Maxwell's mitt, and inserted it into the first baseman's mitt.

"You're not going to catch with that thing, are you?" he asked incredulously.

"Sure," Jarvis replied.

"You'll bust your hand!"

"I don't think so. Anyhow, I'll take a chance."

"All right—get ready for the fast one."

String went through his deliberate wind-up, but this time the arm lashed forward like a cracked whip. There was a sharp smack as the ball hit the center of the glove. The catcher sat on his haunches looking at the horsehide meditatively.

"Hurt?" String asked.

"Nope," Jarvis called, and tossed the ball back.

String grinned. Never had he seen a recruit who

seemed quite so sure of himself. Jarvis *did* know how to handle himself.

"You haven't seen the smoke ball—yet," he promised.

He wound up and uncoiled. The ball burned its way to the light glove, and Jarvis returned it without rising from his crouch.

"Not bad," he called.

"Not bad!" String yelled. "What's your name—Mickey Cochrane or Gabby Hartnett?"

"Jarvis," the catcher replied. "Poke Jarvis!"

"My mistake," String apologized. "Get ready for this one!"

This time String blazed over the lightning-bolt pitch that had earned him nearly as many strike-outs as his curve.

"Peach!" Jarvis complimented.

"Thanks," replied String, slightly irritated. "If I keep on, maybe I'll make the team."

For the next five minutes String put over everything he had—fast balls, curves, pitches that hit the plate, wide ones—and the recruit stopped every ball that could be reached.

As the coach called off the tryout, String walked from the mound to the plate. He noticed the recruit's wide and capable looking hands.

"Where've you caught before?" he asked.

"High school," Jarvis replied, and after a moment's hesitation added: "A minor league pitcher lived next door to us, and I learned something from him."

By the end of the week, it was apparent to String that before the end of the season, Poke Jarvis would be taking his regular turn behind the plate. The recruit had a natural sense of timing at bat, speed on the bases, and a good throwing arm.

The tall pitcher viewed the prospect dubiously. There were reasons why he didn't want to work with a new catcher, this year. His own reasons that he confided only to the picture of Bull Donnelly that hung in the hall just outside of Coach Hendricks' office.

"If I do make the Green Sox," he murmured to Donnelly's picture, "I can afford an Eastern law school. How about it, Bull?"

The level eyes in the picture seemed to smile in affirmation.

On Friday, in the second game of the Tech series, String moved a step closer to his dream. He struck out thirteen men, allowed only one run, and five hits. And when he walked off the mound, his pulses sang with the knowledge that he could have gone a half dozen more innings. He found Poke Jarvis beside him as he strode to the gym, and he put a hand on the recruit's shoulder.

"Well," he said, "you saw a game from the varsity bench. How'd it look to you?"

"Great!" There was frank admiration in Poke's eyes. "I wondered, though—"

"You wondered what?"

Poke's eyes grew puzzled. "Why you handled the Tech shortstop the way you did—in the ninth."

String waited. He had struck out the Tech shortstop.

"He choked his bat," Poke went on, "and he didn't look any too confident. I wondered why you fed him your curve."

String laughed. "What would you have done?"

"Let down on him a little. Lobbed a couple over the outside corner and let him reach for 'em. That way you could have saved your arm."

Save your arm! String laughed. Poke didn't know that he could break a curve as easily as he could pitch a straight ball. Nor did Poke know that the curve was carving out String's career.

"Your suggestion has sense," he said, "and some day, when I'm getting gray and want to last a year longer, I'll remember it!"

String clapped Poke on the back and trotted up the gym steps. Stuff! That's what you had to have to get into the majors! And String felt he was showing the brand of stuff that would compel recognition.

With each passing day, String's spirits mounted. His smoke ball took on added zip. His curves grew sharper. And against Donham U, he struck out nine more. He dressed lazily after the Donham game, reveling in a sense of well-being that left nothing to be desired. And then a voice broke in on his dreams—the serious voice of Poke Jarvis—coming from the other side of the row of lockers.

"Say, Don, I wonder if you'd mind telling me one thing."

The voice of Don Maxwell replied: "Shoot."

"I noticed you let two men steal second on you, and

you hardly bothered to look at 'em. Why was that?"

Don laughed.

"A lot of runners steal second on me."

"You could nip 'em if you wanted to," protested the sophomore. "Get String to deliver the ball a little faster."

"It's simply not our style," Don replied. "We play the batter. If you get the batter out, the base runner isn't going to get very far."

String shut his locker and walked thoughtfully out into the hallway leading to the coach's office. It occurred to him that every game he pitched, the recruit had some minor criticism to make. Probably just airing the baseball knowledge he had picked up from that minor league pitcher. String stopped at the door marked "Hendricks" and opened it. The office was empty.

Aimlessly he wandered about the office, whistling. The coach had told him right after the game to drop in at the office. A slight breeze, floating through the open window, lifted several letters from the coach's desk and wafted them to the floor. String picked them up, and his eyes fell on the third letter. It bore the Green Sox letterhead and was addressed to Hendricks. The first paragraph leaped out at String.

"I'll be down at Southern University for your two-game series," it read. "We're going to have to build up our pitching staff, and the boss has been scouring the colleges. You've got one man—"

String heard steps in the hallway, and moved away from the desk. Coach Hendricks came in, glanced at String, and sat down.

"I called you in to ask you what you thought of Poke Jarvis," the coach said.

"He can catch," String replied, after a moment's hesitation.

"I wish you'd work out with him this week—I think I'll let him catch you in the University series."

String felt a sinking sensation, and grinned to hide it. He'd been expecting this to happen!

"Gosh," he said, "I was hoping you'd let me stick with Don all season."

The coach frowned. "Don's not hitting too well."

"We've worked together so long," String interrupted eagerly. "Why don't you work Poke with Farrell or Bushby—"

"Because one of these days we may need all our strength—against Southern for instance." The coach paused. "Farrell's wild this year and Bushby never was very good. You may have to pitch one Southern game and do relief work in the other, and I may want to use Poke, too."

At the mention of Southern, String's mind leaped to the letter on Hendricks' desk. The Green Sox scout would be there! His heart gave a bound.

"Coach," String said fervently, "you let me pitch to Don and we'll nail that Southern gang to the mast."

The coach laughed. "We'll see," he said. "But you'd better work out with Poke just the same."

String rose to go.

"By the way," the coach said, "take it a little easier from now on. You've been bearing down pretty hard."

"Don't worry," String said cheerfully. "The way I feel, I could work once every day and twice on Saturday."

He walked out into the hall, and glanced up at Bull Donnelly's picture.

"I'll be seeing you one of these days," he promised. "The Green Sox need pitchers."

Two days before the University game, String had a short workout with Poke.

"You may get into a game soon, and you'll want to know my signals," String said. "When I want to throw a curve, I'll give a hitch to my pants. When I want the smoke ball, I'll yank my glove."

There was a look of doubt on Poke's face. "That's all right," he said, "But how about letting me call the pitches?"

"You can," String replied, "but whenever I give either of those two signals, that's the ball that's coming."

Poke's square face grew set. "When I catch," he said, "I like to be something more than a backstop."

String groaned inwardly. He knew now that he had feared something like this ever since Poke had been given a suit. Poke's ideas differed from his, and if he let Poke run the game there was no telling what might happen.

"You've never caught in this league before," he said curtly, "and you'd better let me call the turn when I want to."

Practice was nearly over and String walked away, conscious that Poke's eyes were on his back, and that the recruit's jaw was set.

"A funny kid," String thought to himself. "He's sure he knows more about pitching than I do."

In the seventh inning of the University game, the coach substituted Poke Jarvis for Don Maxwell. Up to that moment String had struck out seven, and State was ahead, 5 to 0.

University's first man up in the seventh was a stocky player who took a short grip on his bat. Patiently String delivered the pitches called for by Poke—two lazy balls over the outside, a fast one inside, and then another slow ball outside, making the count three and one. String fretted over this fooling with a hesitating batter, but his irritation disappeared when Poke called for the smoke ball squarely over the center of the plate. The batter let it go by for a called strike.

"Now the curve," String breathed, "and we'll have him."

But Poke called another pitch over the outside corner, and after a moment of hesitation String gave it to him. The umpire called it a ball and the batter walked.

"That's what you get," String growled to himself, "for playing with a batter."

With the next batter, Poke again refused to call for a curve and finally, with the count three and one, String called for it himself. The pitch broke beautifully and the batter swung six inches over it. String immediately followed with another curve for the third strike.

"That's more like it," String murmured. "Now let's go."

But with the next man up, a notoriously weak batter,

Poke called for a wide one. It seemed useless to String to waste a pitch on a weak man, and he shook his head. Poke signaled again for the wide one, this time insistently.

With a feeling of exasperation, String gave in. With his usual deliberate throwing motion, he aimed for the outside corner of the plate and let go, hoping that it would be close enough for a called strike.

To String's surprise, Poke rose out of his crouch to take the ball, leaped to one side, and lined it to second. String turned to see the runner and ball converging on the bag. There was a cloud of dust as the runner slid, but in the next instant the runner was on his feet streaking for third and the ball was bounding beyond Holden toward the incoming center fielder.

String looked at the runner roosting on third, and a wave of anger swept through him. He walked in halfway to the plate, and waited for Jarvis to come out.

"Didn't Don tell you that we don't play the runner?" he asked, speaking as quietly as he could.

"He did," Poke replied, "but we could have got that man by six feet if you'd thrown a little faster."

"There's no use wasting balls on a weak batter," String replied heatedly. "You can't get men out that way!"

"You can afford to waste one ball to get a runner off bases, can't you?"

String drew a weary breath. Apparently it was no use to argue. No use to remind Poke that men like Grove and Earnshaw ignored base runners and won games.

"From now on," String said, "I'll call the pitches and you stop 'em."

Behind the catcher's mask, Poke's lips were pressed tightly together.

"All right," the catcher said quietly. "Do anything you like."

String walked back to the mound and looked over the batter. A curve and a couple of smoke balls would finish him, he decided. He signaled that the curve was coming, and proceeded to wind up. His side-arm whipped forward and the ball sailed toward the plate.

To String's amazement the curve hit the ground a foot in front of the plate. A sigh of relief escaped him when he saw the bounce land in Poke's mitt.

"I tried to put too much stuff on it," he thought.

He stalled for a moment and then signaled the smoke ball. With the count two and nothing, the batter would probably let it go by. But as String delivered the pitch he was treated to another surprise. The sphere burned its way plateward on a rising slant that carried it high over the catcher's head to the screen backstop. String ran forward to cover the plate, and then stopped, realizing that it was useless. Open-mouthed, he watched the phenomenon of a runner scoring from third on a wild pitch he had delivered.

For the first time that season, String felt shaky. He wiped a trembling arm across his face and walked back to the rubber. The only thing to do now was to get the next ball across. But his pitch was too far inside and the batter walked.

The next man up rapped the first pitch over second for a single. For a full minute String stalled, while the amazed infield called encouragement. At last String decided to try his curve. But the moment the ball left his hand he knew that something was wrong. Big as life, it sailed directly down the groove, without a sign of breaking. The bat came round and there was a crack.

Dumbly String turned to follow the ball. Baker, at shortstop, leaped high into the air. By some miracle he came down with it, and with a quick throw doubled the runner off third for the last out.

The coach was on his feet, his forehead creased, as String came to the bench.

"What happened, String?" he asked anxiously.

String threw his glove to the ground and kicked it to one side.

"I don't know," he replied with a sudden show of temper. "I just can't pitch to Poke, I guess."

"Are you sure that's all?"

"I don't know what else it could be."

The coach thought for a moment. "I can't put another catcher in now," he said finally. "I haven't got anybody. But I can let Farrell finish the game for you."

"You don't have to do that," String replied. "I'll just pitch my own way and let Poke lump it."

Hendricks looked at String soberly, and at last shook his head.

"Nope," he said decisively. "You don't pitch any more today."

String shrugged his shoulders.

"Better go to the showers now," the coach added, "and let the trainer rub that arm."

String was too dazed by his own unbelievable performance to protest. His temper had died, and in its place a cold fear was growing. Was his wildness really due to Poke's stubbornness? Or was it something more serious? Slowly he turned from the coach and walked off the field, unaware of the cheers that followed him.

As he drew near the gym he hastened his steps. He hurried through his shower and rubdown, dressed as swiftly as he could, and strode out of the building, waving a brisk so-long to the trainer.

When he reached the street he sighed with relief. He hadn't wanted to meet the squad, coming in from the field. He didn't want to see Don, the coach, or any of them. He wanted to be alone, to figure out what had happened.

With tentative fingers he explored the muscles of his right arm. He could feel a slight ache there—an ache in one of the muscles of the upper arm, close to the elbow.

"It's nothing," he said aloud. "Nothing at all."

But as he lay in bed that night, gazing sleeplessly at the ceiling, he knew that he could kid himself no longer. He had strained his arm. The throb in his elbow played an impish tune to which String kept repeating two words: "Nothing serious—nothing serious." But he knew that it *was* serious.

During the next week, while the doctor made periodic examinations of his arm, String's hopes gradually began rising. The ache had disappeared and his elbow wasn't visibly swollen. He might conceivably get into shape for Southern in the ten days that remained. Whistling to keep up his courage, he went to Coach Hendricks' office to get the final verdict. In the hall he paid his respects to Bull Donnelly.

"Don't count me out yet, Bull," he said grimly.

The coach was seated at his desk, and he gestured String to a chair.

"The doctor says you can pitch," Hendricks said.

String sat bolt upright, his eyes wide. "Is that straight?" he asked, in a small voice.

"But no more curves," the coach added.

"No what?"

"Throwing too many curves strained your arm," the coach said quietly. "You've got to lay off for the rest of the season."

"But," String blurted out, "take away my curve and you might as well cut off my arm!"

"It's not as bad as that," the coach said. "You've got your control and change of pace—"

String leaped impatiently to his feet. "Who cares about that!" he cried out. "If my curve is out, so am I, and I might as well face it! I'll quit now—"

"Sit down, String." The coach's words were very quiet, but something in his face made String drop slowly into a chair. "Did it ever occur to you that when you abused your curve you were throwing down the school?"

The meaning of the words penetrated to String's whirling thoughts, and he flushed.

"I tried to warn you, but you were sailing along,

chasing a rainbow, and wouldn't listen. Weren't you trying to break Bull Donnelly's record?"

String looked up surprised, and then slowly nodded his head.

"And now that your chance to beat Bull's record is gone, you want to quit cold. Is that it?"

String sat crumpled in his chair, staring at the floor. He hadn't looked at it quite in that way.

"You can still be of service to your team," the coach said. "Even without your curve, you're better than Bushby."

String swallowed. "I'll stick," he said.

On the way to Southern University, State played a two-game series with Leighton. Farrell pitched the first game and won it, but in the second Bushby went sky high. It was State's first defeat of the season, and put her a half game behind Southern.

Two days later Farrell was again on the mound for the first game of the Southern series, and came out on top in a slugging bee, 9 to 7. In the hotel lobby after the game, Coach Hendricks drew String aside.

"Think you can do it?" he asked.

String hesitated before replying. Since that interview in the coach's office ten days ago, he had taken regular light workouts. He had improved his control and had developed a deceptive change of pace. But his fast ball had little hop to it and his curve was forbidden, and without those two weapons he had no confidence.

"I'll do my best," he said, in a subdued tone.

Hendricks looked at String a moment before speaking. "You and Poke have never got along," he said, "but I want you to pitch to him tomorrow. We're going to need his strength at bat. Don didn't make a hit today."

"Poke it is," String replied mechanically.

When String warmed up before the game the next afternoon, he was in a faintly ironical mood. All season he had looked forward to a day like this—a sunny day with a faint breeze, the stands filling with rooters, and a Green Sox scout looking on. The scout was here—a man named Kennedy—but String was no longer interested in him. The only thing in the world he wanted to do was somehow to win this game and keep State in the running for the championship.

As String went to the bench for State's first inning at bat, a thin ray of hope filtered down through his overcast spirit. And the ray came from Poke.

"These fellows have heard about your smoke ball," Poke said, "and they're probably laying for it."

String looked doubtfully at the catcher.

"A man who times himself to hit a fast ball has trouble with a slow one," Poke went on.

A slender ray—but it was something. With a shade more confidence, String watched Baker go to the plate and Tillotson go on deck. The bench started talking it up.

"Come on, you two," Waddey called. "Let's get a few runs!"

"A flock of 'em," yelled Holden.

State started with a rush, intent on giving String a lead. Baker crowded the plate for a walk. Tillotson singled off the first ball pitched, sending Baker to third. Manning grounded out, but Waddey laced a double that cleared the bases. The scoring ended there, but when String walked to the mound for the second half of the inning there was a lump in his throat. His team was in a fighting mood, ready to make it a slugging bee. And they were calling clever encouragement to him as they never had in the days when his curve had made their bats unnecessary.

Southern's first batter was in the box, his eyes on String, his stick held back, and his body bent almost over the plate. Poke signaled for a pitch squarely over the middle, and for a moment String had a feeling of panic. In that instant, he knew that this game was going to be an ordeal such as he'd never faced before. With an effort he mastered himself and threw. The ball cut the heart of the plate, and the batter didn't offer.

Poke called next for a floater over the inside corner, and String lobbed it up. The batter straightened to let it go by, and the umpire called it a ball. Again String lobbed for the inside corner and again the batter passed it up, but this time it was good.

"Strike two!" the umpire called.

The batter showed his annoyance by taking a new toehold at the plate and waving his bat. String gave a slight nod in response to Poke's sign and proceeded to aim a pitch over the outside, low. The batter looked at it, decided at the last minute that it might be good, and uncertainly swung. The ball rolled to the second baseman for the first out.

String wiped a few beads of sweat from his eyes and looked over the second batter. He was a rangy, powerfully built player, and to String his bat looked as big as a tennis racket. Poke was squatting behind the plate, calling encouragement:

"Right over the middle—he can't hit it."

String wound up and delivered his slow ball. The batter shortened his grip and dumped the pitch into the ground for a perfect bunt.

"Never mind that," yelled Poke. "The next two are easy."

In obedience to the signal, String attempted to feed the third man a fast strike past the handle of his bat, but to his dismay he found the ball angling squarely over the middle. There was a loud crack, and the ball sailed out to the fence beyond the left fielder. The man on first raced all the way home and the batter pulled up at second.

"Now the slaughter starts," String said to himself. "Without my curve I'm just another pitcher."

Poke walked out to String.

"Never mind that last pitch," he said. "You grooved it and he was laying for it. Just keep firing at the corners and we'll get this next boy. He isn't tough."

String drew a breath and nodded. "You call 'em and I'll put 'em there."

"That's talking," Poke said warmly.

String barely glanced at the next man. He knew it was Hod Walker, leading hitter in the Conference, and that Walker might well drive one of those limping pitches out of the park. But he resolutely removed the batter from his mind and concentrated on the pitch.

"High and inside," he said to himself. "Here goes."

The pitch went straight to its mark for the first strike.

"He doesn't want 'em there," String said to himself. "He likes to take a full swing."

String put his second one too far outside for the batter to reach, but his third one again cut the inside corner for a strike. Walker swung his bat impatiently.

"He doesn't like 'em, but he knows he may have to hit one," String said doggedly.

Again he aimed a floater inside, and in desperation Walker stepped back and swung. The ball popped off the handle of his bat, and String himself caught it for the second out of the inning.

The pitcher felt a glow of pleasure such as he'd never felt in the days of his devastating curve.

The next man up sent a long fly to Bob Waddey for the third out, and String walked off the diamond. As he sat down he noted with surprise that his hand was trembling.

"Good going," Poke said to him.

"Tough going," String amended.

"It's just a matter of never giving 'em anything good to hit at," Poke said confidently. "If we can't dazzle 'em with speed we'll befuddle 'em with accuracy."

During the second inning, String didn't pitch a single ball over the center of the plate. His target was a rectangle, with Poke's knees and shoulders at the four corners, and he aimed all his pitches at the two sides of the rectangle. Up and down those two edges, first on one side and then the other, now fast, now slow, he did his sharpshooting. And all Southern could get was a scratch single.

But at the end of the inning String knew that if sharpshooting wasn't hard on the arm, it was wearing to the nerves. He felt already as though he had been through a nine-inning game.

In the third inning, his control momentarily broke. The first Southern batter hit a hot grounder to Baker, a shortstop, and Baker proceeded to play jacks with the ball. The second and third men walked, filling the bases.

Rubbing a sweating palm down the side of his pants, String walked forward to meet Poke. The catcher's mouth was set.

"You're losing your nerve," Poke challenged. "Everything you pitch is going just outside. You've got to get back on those corners. You can do it."

"This isn't my game," String murmured shakily. "I've never done anything like it before."

"You did fine the second inning," Poke came back, "and you can do just as well now." He looked around at the three Southern runners populating the bags. "It's a good spot for a double play. We'll let the next man hit."

String looked to see who the new man was. His heart gave a bound as he recognized Hod Walker, up for his second turn at bat. Poke noticed the glance and shrugged his shoulder.

"He isn't so tough," he said calmly. "He likes 'em low and outside."

"How do you know?" String asked unsteadily.

"Because you pitched a wide one to him the last time, and he started to reach for it." Poke was smiling confidently. "Give him the same thing you gave him last time—high ones on the inside."

They parted. Summoning all his control, String fed Walker a floater on the inside. A second and a third one found the same spot, and the umpire called two of them strikes. A fourth one—fast, this time—went to the same mark, and the enraged Walker swung on it. The ball careened off his bat and bounced crazily between third and second. Manning at third dashed to his left to field it, but the sphere rolled out to the grass.

Two men scored. One gleeful Southern man was roosting on third and Walker was at first.

"Horseshoes," Baker yelled derisively.

"We'll get those two back, Poke!"

"Not your fault, String!"

String wet his lips. It was his fault. If he hadn't walked those two men nobody would have scored. His mouth set grimly. He had grown faint-hearted and lost control, but he wouldn't lose control again.

With the next batter, his pitches were again punching holes in the edges of the rectangle, and the man finally grounded weakly to Holden at second for a double play. While the double play was being completed, the man on third scored, and that ended the scoring for the inning.

String collapsed weakly on the bench and closed his eyes. He wondered idly what Kennedy, Green Sox scout, thought of the exhibition.

"Not," he murmured to himself, "that it makes any difference."

He felt a hand on his arm and opened his eyes to find the coach setting next to him.

"You're doing a good job, String." There was warmth in the coach's voice and String smiled appreciatively. He wasn't fooled by the remark—it was a pretty rotten exhibition. But he was grateful, just the same.

"How do you feel?" the coach asked.

"I feel as if I'd gone through the wringer," String replied frankly.

"Is it your arm?"

"No—my courage. I let myself go that last inning." String sat up straight and a new light came into his eyes. "But I'm all right now."

In her half of the fourth inning, State indulged in a batting spree that tied the score at 4-all. And in the innings that followed String stuck steadfastly to his task of keeping the Southern sluggers guessing. In the sixth, the Southern coach on the third-base line cupped his hands.

"Come on, gang!" he yelled, "this boy hasn't got a thing."

String looked at his shoes and smiled. So they'd found it out at last! If it hadn't been for Poke's uncanny signal calling, he reflected, they'd have known it long ago.

After that his job grew harder. The Southerners began stepping back to nail the inside pitches and reaching across the plate to batter the outside ones. In every inning, Southern got men on bases. For String, existence became a succession of pinches, each one of which bruised his spirit and shattered his nerves. Where once he had been able to save himself with a blinding smoke ball or an unhittable curve, he now had to achieve the same end with a floater that cut the corner, or a change of pace that threw the batter off time.

He didn't quite keep Southern from scoring. In both the sixth and seventh innings, Southern got a man across, bringing her total to six runs. But in State's half of the ninth a triple by Manning cleared the sacks and put State one run in the lead, and String walked out for his last inning with the knowledge that Southern mustn't score.

It seemed to String as he faced the first batter that he'd been standing on that mound for a week, and that there was nothing left to him but a ragged loop of raw nerves. Once again he started the painful job of cutting holes in the corners of the rectangle, but after two pitches he knew that his control had gone wobbly. Before he could master himself, he had passed the first batter.

The infielders pelted encouragement at him, but under their cheerfulness String detected a note of strain. He glanced over at the bull-pen, saw Farrell warming up, and felt an overmastering desire to walk to the bench. With an effort he eliminated the thought.

"Poke's calling for a floater," he said numbly. "Another floater."

He loosed the pitch, and with relief saw it going accurately for Poke's left knee. The batter topped the ball to deep short, and String's mind mechanically recorded the fact that a runner was forced out at second.

String's next pitch was just as accurately aimed at Poke's right shoulder, but the batter reached out, luckily connected, and drove the ball between second and third for a single. A fast throw-in by Oberg held the advancing runner at second.

String looked at the men on first and second and felt a familiar pounding sensation in his veins. It was another pinch and he was afraid he couldn't see it through. Then he looked at the plate, and the pounding in his veins increased. Hod Walker was up. String stepped off the mound and beckoned to Poke.

They met halfway to the plate.

"If we need it," String said, "I think I can give you the curve."

Poke looked up quickly, and saw the desperation written in the pitcher's face. Slowly he shook his head.

"My arm feels good," String lied. "And it's almost the end of the game."

"A wild pitch would let in a run!"

"There'll be no wild pitch!" String grasped Poke by the arm. "Remember the signals? If I give you the sign, get ready to catch the curve."

String turned to go, but Poke swung him around. "String," he pleaded. "Don't be a fool!"

String's eyes dropped to the ground and ⌐ passed through his frame. "I'm shot," he murmured, "Completely shot."

"Don't worry," Poke gripped String's arm tightly. "Listen. Can you give me just four more pitches?"

String didn't answer.

"Just four more," Poke said, "and we'll have this man out."

"All right," String said at last. "I'll give you—four pitches."

With a pat on the arm, Poke turned quickly and walked back to the plate. As he passed Walker, he grinned.

"You think you haven't seen any stuff," he said carelessly. "Well—watch this."

Poke crouched behind the plate and signaled for a high one on the inside. The ball sailed over, lazily cutting the corner, shoulder high, for the first strike.

"See it?" Poke said cheerfully, and signed for another one just like it.

Again the pitch came over, but this one was a shade too far in, and the umpire called it a ball.

"What are you doing—kidding me?" Walker laughed. "Stuff!"

"And here's more of the same," Poke said, but this time he called for a fast one right in Walker's groove—low and outside.

The pitch slanted straight for Poke's right knee—the first time that afternoon that Walker had been given a pitch exactly where he wanted it. The batter looked at it in amazement, unable to swing.

" 'Smatter?" Poke laughed. "Didn't you want it?"

For an instant Poke debated over the next pitch. He threw a quick glance at Walker and saw him shortening his grip on the bat. That decided Poke. Walker didn't expect two balls in succession right in the groove. Walker was getting ready to back up and chop at another inside ball. Poke decided to risk everything on a groove ball. He rose from his crouch and stuck out his glove.

The ball came over. Too late, Walker realized that he had been crossed up. With his shortened grip he was unable to swing effectively. All he could do was to reach out and strike weakly at the ball.

By luck he connected. The grounder came to Holden on the second bounce. Holden tossed to Baker, forcing the runner at second, and Baker threw to Todd, completing the double play.

The game was over, and State had won 7 to 6. For a half minute String contemplated the miracle, too exhausted to feel elation or to respond to the pounding his teammates gave him. He was the last to enter the dressing room, and for a moment he leaned wearily against the door.

In the center of the room, Coach Hendricks was talking to a short man with a round, red face. The coach beckoned.

"String," he said, "this is Mr. Kennedy."

String's face took on color. He walked forward and shook hands diffidently. The scout's eyes quickly took in

String's rangy form, his long fingers, and sinewed wrist.

"You pitched a pretty good game, son."

String laughed. If he had counted right, Southern had scored six runs and made 13 hits. And there hadn't been a single strikeout.

"I might have given a better account of myself a few weeks ago," he said, smiling.

"I saw you a few weeks ago." Kennedy's eyes were reminiscent. "I saw you pitch against Donham, and I wasn't much impressed."

"I didn't suppose you would be," String laughed apologetically. But he was bewildered. He had blanked Donham and struck out nine men in the bargain.

"You showed plenty of stuff," Kennedy said, "but no judgment. You weren't deceiving those Donham men. You were overpowering 'em, and you can't do that in the majors. Bull Donnelly tried it."

At the mention of Bull's name, String became interested. "How's Bull coming?" he asked eagerly.

"Bull's burned out," Kennedy replied. "We're letting him go."

"What happened?" String held his breath.

"Threw too many curves," Kennedy said laconically.

String digested the news in silence.

"I was afraid you were headed the same way," Kennedy said. "But today you showed me something. Any man who can keep the hits scattered the way you did, without throwing a curve or a smoke ball all afternoon, has a pitching head."

"You'd better talk to Poke Jarvis, the catcher," String

said slowly. "The headwork was all his. Every single bit of it."

"I had my eye on him," Kennedy said, smiling. "I saw him pull you through. And I think you've learned something. Be sure to let me know your address when you get out of school."

Weariness dropped from String's shoulders like a discarded cloak. The bright vision that had come to him early in the season flooded back in all its brilliance, robbing him of the control that he had so desperately clung to, all during the game.

"I'll—I'll do that," he stammered, and turned suddenly away.

With a light tread he covered the few paces to his locker. He dropped down on the bench, and the face he turned to Poke Jarvis was shining.

"Thanks, Poke," he said.

The Kid from Thomkinsville

John R. Tunis

B y the end of the first week practice was livened by
inter-squad games. The teams went five or six
innings after the regular workout, and consequently the
squad seldom returned to the hotel before two-thirty or
three in the afternoon.

Hopefully the Kid sat on the bench every day. The
pitchers were permitted to go only a few innings and
each morning he waited for the call which didn't come.
Harry Street, his roommate, got in at shortstop for
several innings, however, and made two clean hits in his
two times at bat off Jake Kennedy, the veteran pitcher.
He was a queer youth, quietly confident of his own
ability and his ultimate success.

The Kid would have given plenty for that kind of

temperament. When their lights were out at night and they lay abed discussing the day's play, his roommate always ended on the same note.

"Aw . . . I can hit any right-hander in this-here league. . . ." Then he would turn over and be asleep in five minutes.

Finally, while the Kid sat in the hotel lobby one evening, consumed by doubts, Gabby Spencer suddenly stepped up to him.

"How's 'at ol' arm, Tucker, okay? Yeah? I'll shove you in there tomorrow."

The Kid could hardly sleep all night. At last, a chance against the big league hitters! What he'd been hoping for since he landed in Clearwater, and now that the moment had come he was frightened. Next morning when he came out of the clubhouse, he beheld a strange sight. Half a dozen photographers were snapping Razzle Nugent, the star pitcher. Razzle lay on his back. Above him leaned the trainer rubbing an enormous medicine ball across his stomach. On all sides stood the cameramen, two of them mounted on a packing box, others standing on chairs. Then that piercing whistle called them to practice.

As he walked across the diamond he heard someone say, "Yeah, they're shooting Razzle 'cause this morning he's going in a few innings for the first time."

Nugent was pitching against him! A chance to beat the great Razzle, to bring himself to the attention of the owner sitting there on the clubhouse porch, the newspapermen scattered over the press box, and Gabby himself. If it had only happened ten days before! Now he felt worried and uncertain.

There was the usual warm-up, the pepper practice, and after that he took a few swings at the plate. Then the whistle blew again. Two teams started a game and once more the Kid found himself on the bench, eagerly watching every move, waiting for the call. It came in the third inning when Gabby pulled out Rats Doyle who was puffing and blowing in the hot sun.

From the coaching lines, Gabby shouted, "Hey, there . . . Tucker!"

The Kid jumped. Thump-thump went his heart. He knew Razzle would be sent in for the regulars and already he could see the headlines in the next morning's sport pages. "Razzle Nugent beats Rookie Pitcher." However, he was starting with a three to one lead in his favor, and he walked out to the box hoping desperately that he wouldn't disgrace himself in his first try.

He found pitching to these men very different from any past experience. They had an annoying habit of standing there motionless, their bats on their shoulders, refusing to bite at anything wide, just waiting, waiting . . . and then when a good one came, smacking it. Fast fielding saved him in the first inning he pitched, but when he came out after three innings, the score was eight to three for the regulars. His roommate put on the finishing touch by cracking him for a double to score two men, and then dancing off second and stealing third under the Kid's eyes. It was his fault, entirely, and not the catcher's. He longed for the confidence of that brown-eyed boy jumping off third.

"Watch yourself there . . . watch yourself," shouted the coach back of third as the youngster hopped up and down the basepath, arms outstretched.

"Yeah," retorted the brash rookie, "well, I got here on my own steam and I'll get home on my own too."

A titter went around the diamond at the expense of Charlie Draper the third-base coach. In the box the Kid heard the retort and winced. That was the kind of temperament to have. Meanwhile, Evans, the big burly first baseman, apparently afraid of nothing and known for his ability to hit any sort of ball, stood menacingly at the plate. In desperation the Kid put everything he had into his pitch. He wound up, the batter met the ball, the fielders backed up . . . it was over the fence. He heard the call from the first base coaching line.

"Clancy, let's see what you can do out there." The Kid came back slowly, stuffed his glove into his hip pocket, put on his sweater and walked round behind the plate to the clubhouse. He knew what they were saying in the dugout as he went by. Seven runs, three bases on balls and heaven knows how many hits. In three innings. A knot of men on the clubhouse porch were watching the game and talking. They paid no attention as he passed and he heard someone say:

"If Gabby wasn't a fixture at short I'd say it would be hard to keep that fresh busher off the team." They were talking about Harry, his roommate.

The Kid from Thomkinsville

As he went inside to the showers, typewriters were clattering merrily in the press box beside the clubhouse. The press, anxious to be off fishing, were writing the leads to their daily stories without waiting for the end of the game. Casey was shoving in his last sheet.

The biggest disappointment of the day's play was that peerless leader, Manager Gabby Gus Spencer, at shortstop. If his play today was a sample, Mac-Manus ought to ship him to the minors. An 18-year-old busher named Harry Street had the edge on him.

I've always had a suspicion that Gabby talks a better game of ball than he plays. You can have my share of Gabby if you give me young Street, and I'll throw in Tony Galento and One-eyed Conolly too. With his bunch of sapadillos, Gabby will be lucky not to end up by the Fourth of July in the International League.

He had three pitchers in there this morning throwing the ball all over the park except at the plate, and young Tucker, the sensational Kid who was to pitch the team into the World Series, tried his luck for the first time and delivered up seven runs in three innings.

However, there's one thing about our Dodgers. I'd rather watch them run past each other on the bases and fall asleep at bat than see the Yanks win a double-header without a run scored against them. When the Yanks play you know what'll happen. With the Dodgers, anything can happen. And usually does.

When the Kid reached the hotel tired and discouraged, he found a big pile of mail waiting for him.
Seemed as if everyone in Thomkinsville was writing.
Everyone at home they said, even old Mr. Haskins the
president of the First National Bank who had told him
he'd be unwise to leave his job at MacKenzie's drug-
store, was reading the sports pages in hopes of seeing
his name. Did he think Brooklyn would win the pennant? When was the Kid going to start a game and show
those birds up?

There were a dozen foolish questions in every letter.
He wished they hadn't written at that particular minute.
One after the other, he opened and read them; each one
hurt. Up to a lunch which he couldn't eat, and then to
the beach alone. He returned early to dinner so he
wouldn't have to face the other players. It was after eight
and he was sitting alone in the dark room when a knock
sounded at the door. He leaned over quickly and put on
the light.

"C'm on in . . ."

The door opened and Leonard entered. He saw a
solemn-faced boy hunched up in a chair by the window
overlooking the front porch.

"Hullo there. Thought I'd drop in a minute."

"Uhuh. Sit down, won't you?" Ordinarily he would
have been delighted to see the old catcher, but not that
night. That night he wanted to be alone.

"Well, things didn't go so good out there for you this
morning, did they?

The Kid hadn't wanted even to think about it, but all

of a sudden he discovered a desire to talk. "No, sir. They sure didn't. Don't know why, but I didn't seem to have any control."

The older man nodded. "That's often how it is. Well, it's not the first time you've been belted, I guess, nor the last time, either. Pitching against real hitters is tough, especially at first. You'll get used to them. I think I might have helped you once or twice if I'd been in there. That time you grooved the ball for Evans."

The Kid shook his head. "I thought I'd fool him."

"These boys are too smart." There was a pause. Then suddenly the old catcher leaned forward. "You feel right sorry for yourself, sitting here all alone in the dark, don't you, son?"

Now how on earth did he know that. How did he know the lights had been off? No, the Kid certainly wasn't happy, flopping in his first chance in the big leagues. The visitor leaned back in his chair.

"Well, I'm going to tell you something. An' I mean it. You got the makings of a good player. You can hit, and I think you can pitch. Only one thing. It's up to you."

"Up to me?"

"Yep . . . Like this, now. A fellow gets out of baseball just what he puts into it, understand? Any boy with arms, legs and a good heart can break into the big leagues. I think . . . ah . . . now I think you've got them. Maybe I'm wrong."

Arms. Legs. A good heart.

"But I'm not wrong on rookies very often. Lemme tell you something. Unless he has awful tough breaks, any youngster who's fast and can throw and can stand up to the plate, should make the grade. If he has one thing.

"Y'know, I've seen lots of ballplayers that had everything except courage. They just didn't have that. And they wouldn't work. Pink Benton for instance, back when I was with the Senators, remember him? One of the best rookies ever I hope to see. Young. Strong as an ox. A good hitter, but no dash. Everyone had the tag on him. Just another ballplayer." There was a significant pause again. Then he said dryly, "He's with Fort Worth now."

The Kid began to understand. Before he could answer, the catcher went on. "Take Gabby, right here on this club. Gabby . . ."

That was too much. The Kid had been watching Gabby closely for two weeks, and, despite his poor play that morning, he had respect for the manager's ability. "Say, that guy's one swell ballplayer!"

"Sure he is. Why? How'd he get to be manager? Never hit three hundred in his life. Not too hot in the field. But he's been in the big leagues over ten years now. The answer's easy. Gabby has what it takes. Something inside, if you get me. Full of pepper all the time, and salt too, and vinegar, yes sir, plenty of it. He's scrapped more than the rest of this squad put together."

Gradually the Kid realized what baseball really was, what it took. Here he was sitting in the dark, feeling sorry for himself when he ought to be forgetting what had happened and getting ready for another day. The older man leaned toward him.

"Look at Maranville. The Rabbit . . . never heard of him, hey? You have? Well, there was a little fellow about as big as a peanut, couldn't hit with a tennis racket, yet he was twenty years in the league. And old John McGraw . . . what made him a great player? Same thing—fight. And Frank Chance. Why he used to do everything but walk out there and punch his own team on the nose to pep 'em up. Take Joe McCarthy. Never good enough to be a big-leaguer himself, now look at him. Just scrub he was, once; now everyone wants to be on his team."

The Kid had followed baseball all his life, loved the game, played it, yet for the first time he realized that more important than fielding or hitting was that queer inner quality called courage.

"Know what happened to you this morning?" The catcher tipped back his chair. "Well . . . I'll tell you. You were choking up. Pitching calls for coordination. You didn't have any, and you were going too far back. I watched you carefully; you were throwing with your shoulder so far back it's a wonder it didn't drop off. Now I been through all this the same as you. I sat alone in a hotel room in the dark one night and saw myself with Utica on my shirt, the same as you. Buck up, son. Forget this afternoon. Tomorrow's another day, get out there and play ball . . ."

He walked toward the door. Hand on the knob, he turned round and grinned.

"Good night!" he said abruptly, and went out.

"Good night." The Kid jumped up from his chair. Tomorrow he'd show them. He walked up and down the little room, the words of the veteran Leonard in his ears. To get discouraged, disheartened over one bad inning, that was foolish . . . he wouldn't do that again.

It was the last game of the pre-season workouts and the team was playing the Indians. After that, one more day of practice and then the whole squad would break camp at Clearwater and start the long slow journey north, playing the Yanks every day in a different city and arriving in Brooklyn three days before the season began. As usual during games, MacManus sat on a small wooden chair near the clubhouse porch behind the left field foul line. An empty chair stood on each side of him, and from time to time some old player or one of the sports writers drifted over and sat down for a few minutes.

He was in a happy mood. The Dodgers had won two straight games from the Indians and this one was going well. At the end of the fourth the score stood nothing to nothing and the Indians had not made a hit. It was Razzle Nugent's first game, and he was showing all his old stuff. As the teams changed sides, the umpire turned to the stands.

"Now pitching for Brooklyn . . . Roy Tucker, No. 56 in place of Nugent, No. 37. At short, Harry Street, No. 24 in place of Spencer, No. 4."

A tall man with glasses slipped into one of the empty seats. "Hullo, there, Jack." It was Red MacDonald, manager of the Cincinnati team which had an off day. "Thought I'd drop over and see how you boys were doing. Who's that going in at short?"

"Hullo, Red. How are you? That's young Street. I picked him up in Muskegon last summer. This is his first game in the big time, so he probably won't do much. Just watch him run though. That kid can run, lemme tell you. Say, when I watched him running for hits right in back of second, I offered his manager ten thousand for him on the spot. Speed counts in this game."

"And that tall kid pitching now?"

"Tucker. He's another rookie. I got him in Waterbury, Connecticut. He was pitching one day against the Cuban All-Stars when I went up there to look at Simpson, their shortstop. This Kid held 'em to one hit, and I signed him then and there. He's only nineteen and doesn't know what it's all about yet."

MacDonald spat into the ground. "Well, there he starts to blow . . ."

The first batter for the Indians received a base on balls. The Kid stood in the box with his legs apart as the batter trotted down to first, and old Dave, his catcher, came out to him. Their heads went together a minute and the arm of the other man rested on his shoulder. That steadied the Kid a little, but Davis, the Cleveland next batter, hit a beautiful line drive down the alley between short and third.

"There she goes," exclaimed MacDonald. "There's a hit . . . oh . . . what a stop!" The man on first was well on his way down to second when the shortstop leaped through the air and with a backhand stab snared the ball close to the ground. He rolled over twice, picked himself up and threw to first for a double-play. The ball park roared. Catching the Indians in a double play pleased the crowd.

A minute later the side was out and Street came in, tipping his cap. The Kid squeezed his arm as they slipped into the dugout. "Boy, you sure saved my bacon that time!"

"Yeah . . . now let's go get some runs," said the confident youth, waving his bat. And old Leonard taking off his pads looked up at the Kid. "All right, boy, you put the ball where I told you. What? Sure you had luck, maybe you'll have some more. Keep cool and throw it where I say, that's all."

In left field, MacManus leaned back in his chair, his arms outstretched. He was pleased with himself and the world in general. "Yessir, that kid runs like a leaping gazelle, I'm telling you. Hullo there, Jim . . . how you like him?" This to Casey the sports writer who came over and took the empty chair. "How's that for a stop, hey?"

"Looks as if maybe he might have something. I talked to him last night. Say, he's full of pepper. 'I can hit any right-handed pitcher in this-here league,' he says. 'Oh yeah,' says I, 'well maybe you'll have a chance tomorrow against Ruffing.' 'Okay,' he answers, 'I'll hit him.' How's that?"

"Well, he will, too. And he can bat from either side, remember."

"Can he? He ought to be a ballplayer one of these days. Who's that kid in the box now, Larry?"

"Roy Tucker. Lad from Thomkinsville, I was telling you about him."

"Oh, yeah, I remember. Has he been out all along? I haven't noticed him. And if that hotfoot out there in short hadn't picked up that liner he would have been scored on in the last inning. Now the rookie I like is young Jack Maguire with the Giants . . ."

MacManus' face lost its contented look. "The Giants, the Giants! You sports writers give me a pain. If a man wears a Giant uniform you all think he's hot stuff, and if he's on the Dodgers he's a dud. The Giants . . ." and he snorted as he turned his back to the other man who winked at MacDonald and moved back to the press box.

"The Giants!" MacManus exploded again. "How you making out this year, Red?"

MacDonald thought he had a better team. So did every manager. "Say, Jack, how about Nugent? Think he can come back?"

MacManus became serious again. "Well, we don't know. Just now he's tending to business, and he pitched good ball today. He's promised to cut out the wild stuff and play all season. What's the matter, Red, looking for a pitcher?"

"I could use an extra one. How about this kid in the box there, what'll you do with him?"

"Send him to Nashville, I suppose. Interested?"

"Not especially."

"Like his motion? He's got an easy swing there, hasn't he?"

"Yeah," replied the other man without much enthusiasm. "I like it."

"So do I!" MacManus barked. Someone had been

tipping Red off about the Kid and if MacDonald wanted him enough to come up and watch him play, the boy was worth hanging on to. He turned back to the game. "Hullo, that's two strike-outs this inning. This kid will do all right when he gets some seasoning."

As inning after inning went by and neither team made a hit, MacManus was unable to stand the strain. He rose nervously and walked about for a moment before returning to his chair.

"Yessir, Red," he remarked suddenly, "I got this boy up in Waterbury where he held the Cuban All-Stars to one hit. I said to Spike Davis the manager, I said, 'Look here, I'll give you just exactly ten thousand smackers for that son of a gun right here and now.' And he says, 'Well, that boy has awful big possibilities,' and I said 'Yeah, and so has ten thousand in the bank . . .' Oh, oh! . . . there goes the ball game, Red!"

Rosetti had cracked a terrific drive into center. Scudder, the left fielder, was nearest the ball and went after it, running back and back. He came up against the fence as the ball descended. From the stands it looked over, but the fielder turned, leaped up, and literally pulled it down from the upper boards. It was a courageous catch and the whole crowd rose to applaud him.

"Yessir, he's getting support all right. Well, this is the ninth, and two out. Who's up? Rogers? Say, young Tucker has a chance of shutting these bums out."

The batter took one strike and a ball. He was looking for a fast one, but it was a curve and he swung well over the ball. His bat slipped from his hand, the ball rolling in the dirt toward third. Like a flash he was off while both the Kid and the third baseman ran in for it. The Kid got it, stumbled momentarily, then threw to first, a fraction of a second too late. Hit number one for the Indians.

"Rats!" snapped MacManus. "I hoped the Kid would hold 'em hitless. Would have given him all kinds of confidence."

The catcher went down the line to the box and tossed the ball. There was silence on the diamond. Was this another ninth inning Indian rally? From the infield came the chatter of the team. "All right, now, Roy, old kid, right in the slot . . . Pretty lucky, that was. Give him both barrels, Roy . . ."

Then the voice of the umpire, "Strike ONE . . ."

"Thassa way to throw that old tomato, Tuck, old boy . . . That's pitching!"

A minute later the man on first started for second. Leonard's throw was perfect and the side was out, the Dodgers coming up for the last half of the ninth.

MacManus got up and again walked nervously back and forth.

Leonard was the first man up. He stood swinging his bat at the plate while MacDonald reminisced.

"Old Dave. Still a pretty good catcher that old fella. I remember him back in the Series against the Tigers in thirty-four . . ."

"Yeah," MacManus said. "A long while ago. He's old

now, too old. We want youngsters, and speed, see. Speed, that's to be the keynote of this team. A hustling ball club. Like that kid coming to bat now."

Leonard had flied out, and Harry Street came to the plate. With a base on balls and two hits behind him, he caught the first ball pitched for a clean single to right center. MacManus poked his neighbor in the ribs.

"How's that, Red? Batting 1000 in his first big league game. If that kid was with the Giants, you can imagine what they'd say!" With a decisive gesture indicating his opinion of sports writers, he sat down again. Silent but keen, MacDonald watched while MacManus twitched and crossed his legs.

"Jack, I'd just as lief make an offer for that pitcher if you'd care to listen."

"Nossir!" MacManus barked. "That kid has got something, Mac. I'd be a fool to let go of him."

The batter lashed a fast grounder to shortstop and Street darted toward second. It was plain that only an exceptionally fast throw would catch him, and Mac-Manus half rose in his chair.

"They'll have to be fast!" he shouted exuberantly. "They'll have to be fast to get him . . . there . . . I told you . . . I told you . . ." as Street slid safely into second. "Wha' d' I say? He's a leaping kangaroo, that's what he is. Now, Kid, let's see you win your own game."

From deep left field the two men watched the tall, gangling boy step up to the plate. He knocked the dirt from his spikes nervously, gripped his bat well up the handle, and stood, legs apart, on the edge of the box.

"Makes you think of Ted Williams, doesn't he?" said MacManus. From the dugout and coaching lines came the chatter of the Dodgers, "Attaboy, Tuck, take a cut at it . . . You can hit it, Roy, old kid . . . Make him come in there, make him come in, thassa boy . . . Knock his turkey neck offen him, Roy . . ."

He heard their voices as he faced the ball. At last he was getting somewhere. He was one of them, not an outsider any more, but someone for whom they'd leap into the air and risk their necks by barging at full speed into the outfield fences. The late afternoon sun beat on his burning neck as he watched the pitcher wind up and saw his leg rise. The ball was outside and low, but not too far. He leaned against it and felt the tingling sensation of wood against ball.

The crowd rose with a yell. It was a hit, a long hit. Already Street was rounding third, head down and digging, while out in left field MacManus was dancing up and down.

"Hey, Red, how about it? No sir, I'm not selling that kid, not a chance."

Street crossed the plate, as the Kid rounded first. There the young pitcher was surrounded by small boys who suddenly appeared from nowhere and by fans pouring out of the bleachers. Some of the Indians, running toward their dugout, paused to shake his hand. From every side people were patting him on the back.

In the press box the rat-tat-tat of typewriters and the tap-tap of the telegraph bugs picked up speed. Casey tore up a lead he had written before the game and put a fresh piece of paper into his machine. "Now whadye think of that, Tom, shut out by a rookie . . . one hit, too!"

By Jim Casey

The Dodgers have uncovered a pitcher at last. A nineteen-year-old rookie, Roy Tucker, from Thomkinsville, Connecticut, pitching his first big-league game, went for six innings against the Indians here at Clearwater Park this afternoon, allowing one base on balls and one hit, of the scratch variety, struck out seven men, and pitched only twenty-six called balls. No, you don't have to believe it, this is a free country, but four thousand fans watched the Kid hold the Injun sluggers helpless as he hurled his fast ball at the command of veteran catcher Dave Leonard . . .

Half an hour later the squad climbed into the bus to take them back to the hotel. The Kid was tired but wonderfully happy as he waited for the last slow dressers to clamber aboard. There was laughter and shouting and horseplay up and down the bus, everyone calling to him, yelling back at him and using his first name. The day before he was another one of those rookies, now it was, "That's pitching, Roy!" and "Boy you sure turned the old heat on them babies, Roy!"

The bus started off slowly. Doc Masters, the trainer, asleep in his seat, snored gently. Someone reached over and extracted the cigar case from the pocket of his coat.

Half a dozen players helped themselves and then the case was replaced with care.

"Hey, Doc, have a cigar. Have a cigar, Doc?" He woke as the bus swerved round the corner. Sleepily he reached into his pocket to find his case empty, while they laughed and shouted at him, a happy bunch of boys. He grinned and shook his head. Kidding was all part of the game.

From his seat in the rear the rookie who had arrived listened to the talk and laughter. "Condition . . . why you couldn't get in condition if you was to run from here to Los Angeles . . . hey, Fat Stuff, wanna shoot some pool tonight . . . oh, Dave, what about those two bucks you bet me you'd get a hit today . . . I says to him, spring training is the toughest part of it . . ."

Spring training the toughest part of it! He really believed it then, but one steaming day later in the summer, in Cincinnati, he wondered whether it was really so, after all. The bus swung up in front of the Fort Harrison.

"All right now, you guys," bellowed Gabby Spencer. "Everyone dressed for practice tomorrow at ten-thirty. Ten-thirty, remember." The Kid stepped out, surprised to find himself terribly lame. Stiff and lame all over, but happy and content.

"See, like this." Old Dave squatted down in front of the Kid's locker. "See, my right leg keeps the sign hidden from the first base coach, and the mitt, like this, screens it from third. All right. Now the only ones that can see it are you and the shortstop. Now when there's a runner on second, I use a switch signal. Understand . . ."

The Kid, seated on the bench before his locker with nothing on except his inner socks, nodded solemnly. He was dazed by the rapidity of it all. Two weeks before he was in Clearwater, just another rookie about to be sent to the minors for a tryout; now he sat in the dressing room at Ebbetts Field in Brooklyn, ready for his first test in the big league.

Even in a pre-season game no National League team had been able to trim the New York Yankees for some time, but the Dodgers, a last place club the year before, had beaten them two out of five times in the exhibition games on the way north and had taken another game in Brooklyn. So far the Kid hadn't been called on, but he thought he might be told to work a few innings that afternoon. When Dave came across the room he was certain of it.

"Now when I give you the switch signal by touching my mask," the veteran catcher continued, "It means that one-finger-along-the-knee sign for a fast ball is really a curve, and the other way round. Get it? Some boys don't seem to be able to remember signs at all, but you . . ."

"Oh, I getcha all right. But how about shaking you off?" the Kid said, pulling on a white undershirt and drawing up his trousers.

"Well . . . use your judgment. Sometimes I like for pitchers to shake me off. Doesn't mean I'll always change the sign, mind you, but I like to know my pitcher's doing some thinking for himself. If you feel in some particular case you can do better with a curve than the fast one I've called for, say so. Okay?"

The Kid nodded. He leaned over to lace up his shoes, listening carefully all the while with his heart thumping. Yep, they were sure going to use him . . .

". . . See, I just try to work with the pitcher, and take as much strain off him as possible. Don't bother about me; I want you to fix your attention on that there guy at the plate. Two great things in a pitcher are control and confidence. Take old Fat Stuff over there; he hasn't got a very fast ball, but he has a change of pace and confidence. Also he's got a great big heart."

Squatting on the floor he looked up suddenly as the Kid put a generous supply of chewing gum in his mouth. That glance went home.

"Getcha . . ." he nodded.

"Now these boys we're playing today," Dave continued. "They're good batters, sure, but most every good batter has some weakness. Take DiMag. Now when I was with the White Sox his first year we had a pitcher named Dietrich could get him out every time by pitching low. Fact. We got him every time for three games in a row, and then one day . . ."

"What'd he do then?"

The catcher laughed. "I hate to tell you. He got to a low ball and smacked it for one of the longest hits I ever saw. When he comes up, well, keep 'em high and inside to him. And pray. He isn't hitting so good yet anyhow, it's too early for him. Now about this man Dickey. There's a

dangerous batter. Keep it away and outside. Rolfe? Well
. . . a change of pace sometimes fools him badly. Let's
tease Gordon on a slow, outside ball. If he connects, why
we'll try something else.

"One thing more. If you get ahead, keep bearing
down. This boy Nugent lets up, passes a couple of men
as soon as he gets ahead, becomes careless and loses a
game he oughta won. The boys don't like it. Keep
bearing down all the time."

The Kid was nervous. Little beads of sweat appeared
on his forehead as the catcher rolled those great names
over casually, DiMag, Rolfe, Dickey, but though the idea
of facing the best team in baseball appalled him, that
friendly face and those smiling brown eyes reassured
him. If he did go in, Dave would be there behind the
plate, coaching him along. There was a twinkle in those
eyes which radiated confidence.

Suddenly a door banged. Gabby entered red-faced
and perspiring.

"Now then . . . you men . . ." he rasped. The room
instantly became alert. Gabby was a slave driver, and
when he talked, they listened.

"Last game now, you fellas. We beat those babies
three times and Mac is awful anxious to lick 'em again
today. I want you all in there scrapping, and I want
plenty of holler . . . and bite, too. Remember you can't
get a hit with your bats on your shoulders, and you can't
get runs going to sleep on the bases. Jake, I want you
and Rats and that Kid, where is he, young Tucker . . .
oh, there you are . . . I want you fellas to warm up . . ."

118

The Kid felt as if everyone in the room were looking at him. Almost everyone was, too. Yep, he was going in! He flushed as faces turned his way, and hardly heard the bitter-sharp words of their leader.

". . . c'mon now, gang, pour on some pepper out there . . . let's go!"

Snatching their gloves from benches and lockers, the squad turned toward the door. Clack-clack, clackety-clack, clack-clack, their spikes sounded on the concrete runway from the dressing room to the field.

The crowd staggered him. It was a warm Saturday afternoon in mid-April, and spring sunshine flooded the diamond. Ordinarily he would have been anxious to pitch, but the mob which jammed the lower stands, peered over from the second story and even filled the bleachers in left-center was terrifying. He had never seen such a crowd before, and as he warmed up between Jake and Rats Doyle, he felt suddenly weak.

"Gosh, Rats, how many does this park hold?"

Chewing energetically, the man beside him wound up, threw the ball and grunted between his teeth. "Oh, thirty-eight thousand. Forty maybe."

Forty thousand watching a game! The fans were in good humor. They shouted to Swanson the centerfielder who had won yesterday's game with a double in the ninth, they yelled to Gabby Gus as he pranced round short, to Red Evans the first baseman.

"Say . . . Rats . . . I'm sure glad I'm not starting today. Front of that gang . . ."

"What's the difference, boy. Crowds don't mean a

thing. You'll get used to 'em soon enough." He wound up and threw the ball. "Some guys hate it when the gang's out there, but me, I don't like to play to empty stands. This-here-now-crowd all steamed up-like, makes me feel I want to go."

Funny, thought the Kid. Imagine a man anxious to get out there against the Yanks in front of those packed stands. The crowd was still coming, and certain queer insistent shouts arose from the bleachers.

"What's that yelling, what are they hollerin' about, Jake?"

"Them's the loyal rooters back of first. They want young Street to go in. They're hollering for Gabby to shove Street in . . . at that he might let the boy have a few innings today."

Then the bell clanged and the Dodger fielders rose from the dugout to take the diamond as the three pitchers walked in. Gabby came toward them.

"Whaddye say, Tuck, old boy? 'Bout ready?"

"Who? Me? You want me . . . want me to *start* in there, Gabby?" He looked for Jake, but his waddling form was nearing the dugout, pulling on a sweater, his chunky legs churning the ground. Jake and Rats must have known all the time. The Kid was seized with a terrible fright. Why, he'd make a fool of himself . . .

"Sure I want you in there. Remember, this is just an exhibition. Get out and do your best; never mind the crowd, they're pulling for you hard."

The Kid yanked his glove desperately from his hip pocket and started toward the box. Someone slapped him on the back and ran past into the field . . . Harry

Street! Harry was playing short in place of Gabby. A roar greeted him as he neared the mound for the fans were anxious to see him even if he wasn't anxious to see them. Nervous, uncertain, he rubbed the ball in his hands and threw it. Dave Leonard stood smiling behind the plate. The first ball was high and wide, but the second burned across and the old catcher grinned as he tossed it back. The Kid put more into the next and the next. Now his confidence was returning. Leonard nodded, he nodded back.

MacManus was tired. He had flown out to Kansas City to see a young third baseman play, jumped another plane to Nashville the same night for a conference with his farm manager, taken the air again to return to New York, been grounded in Pittsburgh in a storm, and reached Brooklyn by train early that morning. But no one would have guessed he was tired. Apparently he had as much vitality as ever, sitting behind his desk attending to a hundred details; now leaning back in his chair and tossing his horn-rimmed glasses on the desk, now yanking his feet back suddenly to the floor, pressing the buzzer, reaching for the telephone, bringing it down, and pounding his fist to emphasize a point to the visitor in front.

Seated with him was Jim Casey, who, after a few innings of the game had dropped into the office to watch the fiery owner's reaction to the latest insult of his rival, the Giants' manager.

"No, I haven't seen a paper, and what's more, I've got nothing to say . . . nothing . . ."

But Casey knew his man. He continued as if he

hadn't heard the last remark. "Murphy was sounding off yesterday when he heard you won the game against the Yanks in the tenth. Said he guessed the Dodgers must be pretty good. Said the team that beats Brooklyn will win the pennant this year."

A flush of red came over the other's face. He half rose, leaning over toward the sports writer and pounding the table. "Why . . . why that big . . . say, those Giants will be lucky to keep ahead of Philadelphia. And you can say I said so, too. Lemme tell you something . . ." The telephone interrupted him. It was a long conversation and when he had finished the sports writer changed the subject. He had secured just what he'd come for.

"Seems to me, Jack, as if this fogger out there might turn into something. He seems to have pretty good control for a rookie."

"Yeah . . . yeah he may be a ballplayer in a couple of years. Know how I happened to land him? I was up in Waterbury after . . ." The telephone buzzed again.

"Uhuh . . . put him on . . . hello, Tom . . . he did . . . it is . . . okay . . . keep me posted . . ." A steady roar came from outside which penetrated the quiet little room. "Fine. Well, I think he ought to stay in, but Gabby'll have to use his own judgment."

He turned with a satisfied grin.

"Nothing to nothing, end of the seventh, and the Yanks haven't had a man on second yet . . ."

Out on the field the Kid tipped his cap as he crossed the first baseline toward the dugout. He knew they were cheering his pitching, so he touched his cap awkwardly and hurried in as fast as he could. All up and down the long bench came warm-hearted words, often from friends and often also from men who were trying for the same position, who saw themselves shunted off to the minors or even out of a job if he kept on as he was going. Nevertheless they meant what they said.

"You're up after Swanson, Tuck," someone called.

As he reached for his favorite bat, a roar rose from the stands. It was a long clean hit deep into center, and as the fielders scurried for it, the batter, head down, rounded first and started for second. The roar changed into a groan, followed by applause. The New York fielder had nabbed the ball out by the fence, shutting out a sure threebase hit.

Disgusted, the batter turned back toward the dugout. "Nuts . . . that was robbery . . ."

The Kid walked up to the plate amid scattered applause. From behind, in the dugout, and on the coaching lines came calls for a hit. He yanked his cap down over his eyes and waited. The first ball caught the outer edge . . . a strike. Cries of derision came across the infield as, face flushed, he stood watching the motionless man on the mound. This one he'd hit. If it was any good at all he'd clout it . . .

Nearing first he caught Charlie Draper waving him frantically on. He came into second standing up, rounded the base and started for third, when he saw Gabby on the coaching line yelling him back. Digging in his spikes he slid to a stop, turned, and retreated toward second. The ball came swift and low to third, and he would have been out even with the best of slides. Standing triumphantly on second he watched the pitcher and catcher consulting between home and the box, their heads together. That was the same pitcher, he reflected, who had won two World Series games the previous fall.

The crowd was standing to yell and the noise warmed him all over. Now they'd have to keep him. They couldn't send him to Nashville or some farm team now. His mind went back a month when, lonesome and homesick, he looked forward to a chance with Nashville as the greatest possible success to be obtained. Today Nashville would have seemed failure. Funny how a few weeks changed the picture.

Behind Gabby three photographers were kneeling to catch him if he rounded third for the plate, to snap him, the Kid from Thomkinsville who'd shut out the mighty Yanks for seven innings without a hit.

Nothing to nothing, the end of the seventh, and Karl Case, a good steady hitter, at bat. This might well be the winning run. Never had he felt surer, never more confident. Instead of tiring as the game went on, he retained complete mastery of the ball, and knew he could pitch all afternoon that way if only Davy Leonard stood there, steady and helpful at the other end.

Case stood waiting. The Kid returned to life, danced off the bag, watched the pitcher turn and eye him, darted back as the shortstop veered toward the base. Two balls. One strike. Three balls. Four. Case flung his bat toward the dugout and started for first.

Red Evans approached the plate swinging his bat lustily. Now, thought the Kid, be ready, Red will hit it. But all the time in the back of his mind was the one big thought; shut them out, shut them out, shut them out . . .

Bang. The whole field was running. Everyone was running and everyone was shouting. It was a hit to deep left center and the Yankee fielders were after it. The Kid dug in his spikes, feeling sure he would score, when suddenly as he rounded third an enormous yell came to him. Roscoe, the man who caught that first hit had made another impossible catch! Their rally was cut off and that one-run lead which looked so big was still to be made.

The Kid slowed down as the fielder hurled the ball in. Then there came a queer shout. The second baseman stood on the base with arms reaching for the ball. Gabby's face had turned purple.

Big Bill Hanson, the business manager, burst into the room where MacManus and the sports writer were together. He was excited and out of breath as he talked and the man behind the desk yanked his feet to the floor with a jerk.

"The deuce you say!"

"Yeah, well that's how it is with rookies. Shutting out the Yankees seven innings straight was too much, I guess. He must have been dreaming himself into the World Series. Say, I never hope to see a man as mad as Gabby. He swears he yelled, 'Two out, get back, get back!' right in the boy's face. Gabby sure was fit to be tied. 'You big useless busher,' he shouted, 'don't you know yet how many outs in a baseball game?' And you should have seen the Kid's face. He could have made third easy enough, after the catch, and with Scudder up most likely he would have scored. The way he was going those Yanks would have been out there waving their bats until tomorrow morning."

"That's Yankee luck. Too bad he had to be taken out. Well, Gabby knows his stuff."

"Gabby yanked him quick as a flash and slapped a fifty-dollar fine on him. The poor boob was so flustered he didn't know what to say or how to take it, and the gang, half of 'em wanted to laugh and the other half felt kinda sorry for the boy. Then Jake went in and they got out their bats and started hitting him all over the park. Gabby's madder'n ever."

"Dumb work all right," admitted MacManus. "Well, rookies are like that. They all make a lot of mistakes. Don't worry. I'd like to have grabbed that game, but we can't win 'em all."

Opening Day

Jim Brosnan

O n a late-winter day in an old Southern town the Bruins opened their 45th camp for hopeful pros. At noon the air was as warm as a Northern-city summer. Tommy James took a deep breath, sniffed the orange-blossomed air and sat back to enjoy the ride to the camp. Pulling the taxi to a stop, the cabbie said, "Here's where the Bruins play."

Work, you mean, fella. Pros don't play baseball. Didn't everybody know that?

Johnny Story, the scout who had signed Tommy James to a contract had told him, "First thing Giff will do is run your legs off. You like to run, don't you, Tommy?"

Tommy had nodded, a moronic smile on his face. That's what his father thought anyway.

"You're running away, son. From yourself. From your family, from responsibility. You know that, don't you? Baseball's just a game!"

Well, nuts to that noise, Tommy thought. He hefted his suitcase and walked into the camp. A sign on the whitewashed archway gate said: SPRINGTIME HOME OF THE BRUINS. OK. So I'm a Bruin. Nothing to be nervous about. I'll walk up to old Giff and say, "Skip, I'm your new right fielder." Then I'll go out and prove it.

A white-pebbled path led through a stand of skinny pine trees to a long, low building that looked like a converted Army barrack.

There was no one in sight as he walked along the path. He stumbled, banging his knee against the heavy suitcase. His back was still stiff from the long trip. A fat lump rose in his throat.

"Relax!" he told himself. No matter what happened he was still ahead of the game.

Johnny Story had offered Tommy $30,000 to sign a contract. His father, Judge Ivor James, had laughed at their idea.

"Tom will go to college. He's going to be a lawyer," said the judge.

"He'll get married, raise a family and lead a normal life," said his mother.

"What does Tommy say?"

"Nobody asked me," Tommy said "Nobody ever *asks* me. They just tell me what to do!"

"You'll do what's best for you," said the judge. "We'll decide that."

"Good-bye, Mr. Story," said Mrs. James.

The whole conversation took five minutes of an early

autumn day. It echoed in Tommy's mind for five months. He walked to the university each morning, sat in the freshman classes, walked home, ate supper politely and never heard another word.

On February 15 he called Story.

"I'm ready to sign."

"What does the judge say?"

"They don't know about it. I was 19 yesterday. I'm old enough to make my own decisions."

"OK, boy. I've never kidded you, have I? Pro ball's not an easy life. You gotta love it to live it. You know what you're getting into?"

Mrs. James cried when Tommy told them at supper what he'd done.

The judge scowled but said nothing.

"We don't want to stop you from doing what you feel you have to do, son," he said, "I think you're making a mistake, but I guess you're old enough to learn that for yourself."

"I'm 19," Tommy said. "I've got a ticket to Florida. I'm leaving tomorrow."

"All right. Go then."

Tommy reached the end of the path before he became aware of the man on the barrack's steps. Standing there eating an apple was Al Cochran, the veteran Bruin right fielder.

Tommy cleared his throat and asked, "Could you tell me how I find where my room is?"

"Buddy, there's no *room* in this camp for you."

Cochran pointed back over his shoulder but kept his eyes on Tommy's face. "You get a bunk, just like me, in a barrack like this."

"You mean the Bruins live in a barrack?"

"Down here all Bruins are equal—off the field." Cochran waved at the light towers beyond a grove of trees. "Over there, in the ball park, they separate us men from you boys."

He took the bag from Tommy's right hand, held out his own big hand, gripped Tommy's firmly, and said, "I'm Al Cochran. You must be the bonus kid. Right? OK. You come with me. The bunk next to mine will be yours. We're gonna have to keep an eye on you."

"Not many guys here yet," Tommy said, looking down the room at the empty bunks.

Cochran went on. "Everybody else should be in here by tonight. Everybody but Buster Bowman. He's holding out again. Ol' Buster likes to give the front office a hard time."

That night Tommy lay awake for a while. Organized Baseball! Tommy James, organization man! Wonder if they've got me filed by letter or by number. Me, a $30,000 outfielder, college dropout, runaway, ambitious but headstrong, not homesick but a little lonesome.

Tired, Tommy slept.

Manager Giff Browne greeted each player who entered the Thomson Field Clubhouse the next day. Browne, a bouncy little man with a weather-wrinkled face, looked Tommy James up and down, tapped him on the chest with a pudgy finger and said, "Well, boy, you got the size anyway." He smiled and shook Tommy's hand. "Glad to have you with us, James. Get dressed and let's go to work."

The locker with TOMMY JAMES stenciled above it contained two uniforms, one gray, with JAMES in blue letters across the back of each shirt. Three heavy wool undershirts hung on a wire in the back of the locker. A pair of long white sanitary hose lay on top of a pair of outer stockings. A second pair of stockings hung from a hook next to a cap with a B on it.

Tommy emptied the duffel bag in which he'd brought his baseball glove, spiked shoes, athletic supporter and windbreaker. Al Cochran, dripping wet from the whirlpool tub where he had been soaking as Tommy entered the clubhouse, asked, "Say, kid, haven't you got an old pair of spikes? Those new ones will murder your feet."

"I left my other pair at home. They were pretty beat up."

"What size?"

"Eleven."

"Too big. Mine are 10's. We'll have to find you a pair. Maybe Bowman's will fit. His stuff is in that locker next to yours. He left it with the clubhouse man at the end of last season."

"I couldn't wear his shoes without asking him."

"Try 'em on. If he doesn't like it, I'll pinch his head off. You gotta watch out for blisters the first couple of days. Break those new shoes in gradual like. You're only as good as your feet in this game."

Giff Browne had warned them in a short speech before the morning workout, "First-place money in this league is worth $5,000. I don't settle for anything but first. First-class ballplayers and first-class effort. Tomorrow morning you're all going to be stiff. The next day you're gonna be sore. The next day you're going to hate my guts. But on opening day you're all going to be in first-class condition."

Franklin (Buster) Bowman held out for 10 days, a personal record for the ace left-hander. Bowman never signed his contract or reported on time with the other pitchers. A lanky, sinewy man, he said he didn't need seven weeks to get in shape to pitch the opening-day game.

His noisy entrance into the clubhouse barely hid his usual sour springtime disposition.

"Hiya, Giff!" he yelled as he passed the manager's office. "Buster's here. You can start the season now!"

Al Cochran, sitting at his locker, grinned. "The big man's here at last," he said. "What do you say, ace!"

Bowman ruffled Cochran's hair as he walked by him and tossed his straw hat into the locker between Cochran and Tommy James.

"Big Al! Fat as ever, ain't ya. Think you'll be in shape for the opener?"

Cochran's grin faded. "I'll be ready when you are, ace."

"I'm ready, baby. Gimme the ball."

Bowman sat down, reached into his locker, unzipped

his dusty duffel bag and tossed out three left-handed gloves and three pairs of shoes.

"Pair of spikes missin'. Hey, clubhouse man!"

"I've been using them, Buster," Tommy said.

"Don't call me Buster," he said. "It's Mr. Bowman. Who said you could use my shoes?"

"He had just one new pair," Cochran interrupted. "I told him to try your old ones till he broke his in. You're the same size."

"Tommy James!" Bowman said with a sneer. "Bonus baby! Baby's got nothin' but new shoes, huh?"

"Lay off, Buster," Cochran said as he pulled a rubber shirt over his head. "The kid didn't ruin your shoes."

A malicious grin split Bowman's face. "Listen, rookie, let's make a deal. Now you ain't nothin' till I say so, see, but this club give you $30,000 just to *sign* a contract. Imagine that!"

Bowman turned to Cochran. "Big Al, did you know I pitched pro ball for five years and didn't make 30 grand?"

Turning the shoe over in his hand, he pointed it at Tommy. "These shoes you been usin', rook, don't look like much either. So I'll give 'em to ya for 50 bucks. Whaddya say?"

"No thanks," Tommy said. Embarrassed, confused, Tommy could not figure out whether Bowman was being nasty or just kidding. "I'm an outfielder, not a pitcher."

"Thank God for small favors!" Bowman said. "You know, don't you, rook, outfielders ought to pay to get into the ball park. Well, rookie outfielders are in a class by themselves—*third* class, rook. The next time you put on a pair of Buster's shoes you make sure you're old enough to fill 'em."

Red-faced, Tommy walked away, Cochran trailing uneasily behind him.

"Forget it, kid," Cochran said. "Buster's all right. Very even disposition. Always mad at the world."

Tommy should have known he was in for a rough day. Bowman's antagonism was contagious. No matter what Tommy did, wherever he turned, somebody got on him. When he yawned once during calisthenics, Giff Brown, who was just passing by, yelled, "Get your sleep at night, James! We got work to do out here."

Then there was always Long John Mackey. Every time Tommy stepped into the batting cage, he had to listen to the caustic criticism of the batting coach.

"I like the way you swing the bat, James," Mackey had said the first day. From then on he picked Tommy's batting style apart.

"Get your right hand out front. You're pushing the bat. You got a lazy swing. Pop those wrists. Fast hands! Fast hands!"

"Where'd you learn to bunt! Let the ball hit the bat, boy! You're not tryin' to knock it out of the park!"

Tommy stepped back, spit on his hands, dug into the batter's box and tried to remember all of Mackey's advice. Bowman's first pitch headed right for Tommy's shoulder. He jumped back, his cap fell off, and he didn't even see the ball curve over the plate.

Mackey chortled, then said disgustedly, "That was a curve ball, rook. Better keep your eyes open. The big boys throw a lot of 'em."

The monotony of spring training began to douse Tommy's spirit. The daily workouts—there were no days off—had at first just tired him physically. He slept, dreamless and refreshed, 10 hours each night. The days seemed longer and longer, his ignorance appalling. He needed help, wanted it, but they gave it to him in such large doses he couldn't absorb it.

Effortlessly the veteran pros ran through the motions. Uneasily Tommy followed them, sometimes matching stride, swing and throw. They regarded his successes with indifference, his mistakes with contempt. How could he be worth so much and know so little!

Maybe the judge had been right. Maybe all he had done was run away. From home where they told him what to do and when to do it. From school where they told him things he didn't yet want to know. From his future, a lawyer's degree, a solid respectable job.

Tommy didn't want to work like a lawyer; he wanted to play, like a big-leaguer. Big-league ball was obviously not child's play. Signing a contract hadn't made him a pro. Just wearing the uniform didn't make him a Bruin. A guy had to wear one out before he was accepted.

Even Al Cochran, who had been like a big brother to him, couldn't help Tommy in his sorry-for-myself mood.

"Look, buddy," said Cochran, "I got my own problems. If I don't lose five pounds this week, Giff's gonna

135

fine me 50 bucks a pound. And if you think he's been
tough so far, wait till he blows his stack!"

Buster Bowman needled Tommy unmercifully.

"Rook, you're as green as the wood in a Little Leaguer's bat!"

"Bowman makes me feel 10 years younger," Tommy
complained.

"Wish I was," said Cochran. "Don't let him put you
down, buddy."

"Maybe I ought to give it up, Al," said Tommy.
"Maybe I ought to be back in school."

"What's the matter, buddy? You're learnin' all the
time, ain't you? Wait till we start playin' exhibition
games. Get a couple base hits and you'll be on top of the
world."

The Bruins won their first three games. Tommy
spelled Cochran in right field, playing a total of six
innings, batting three times. His only hit, a double,
drove in a run in the ninth inning of the third game.

Giff Browne told reporters, "Keep your eyes on this
boy James. He looks like he might help the Bruins in
the near future."

One reporter asked Al Cochran, "You think the kid's
after your job, Al?"

Cochran laughed. "I might as well pack up and go
home! But listen, Tommy's gonna be all right. Great
prospect. Swings the bat good, and for a big boy he can
really fly! Must go down to first under five seconds,
anyway. Reminds me of when I was that age."

The reporter giggled. Cochran, at 225, was a lumbering buffalo on the bases.

Tommy was elated with his first base hit as a pro.

"Let's go to town, Big Al, and celebrate!"

"See, buddy. I told you. All you need's a little experience. Gets in your blood, this game does."

"That pitcher threw the ball right by me on the first pitch," Tommy said.

"Yeah. He's fast all right. But it's the same problem every time. You gotta concentrate harder, that's all. Quick hands! Quick hands! That's what you need."

"You remember your first hit, Al?"

"Buddy, you never forget the first one."

"Is it worth celebrating?"

"Sure. Let's go."

St. Augustine is ancient, as American cities go. The Spaniards built it in 1565. The soft wind that blows through the town smells of green trees and orange blossoms and salt air from Matanzas Sound where construction of an old fortress was started in 1638. It still stands, surrounded by a wide moat, protecting the city from hordes of tourists who drift through the narrow streets taking snapshots of what used to be the ancient slave market, the Spanish quarter, and the house that is supposed to be the oldest in the country.

Cochran and Tommy walked from the barrack to the Ponce de Leon Hotel.

"I think I'll drop in here," said Cochran.

"I think I'll go to that old fort," said Tommy, "before it gets too dark to see anything. See you later."

"Curfew's midnight, kid. Growin' boys need 10 hours' sleep!"

Tommy glared at Cochran's departing figure.

"Big man!" He muttered to himself. "Let's hear what you call me when I take your job away opening day."

The sea breeze after sunset chilled the air. Tommy climbed upon the wall of the old fortress, holding onto the snout of the cannon that pointed toward the Atlantic Ocean. A small pyramid of iron balls stood next to the gun. Tommy reached over to pick up the top ball. It was welded to the others in the pile.

Wonder how fast this old baby could pitch these balls? Tommy thought, smiling as he ran his hand along the barrel of the cannon. He picked up a loose stone and tossed it over the moat below the fortress wall. Darkness came in rapidly from the east as Tommy walked away.

An ice-cream parlor across the square from the Ponce de Leon gleamed brightly. *I owe myself a milk shake anyway,* Tommy thought.

Sucking the malt from a straw, he glanced through the window and saw Buster Bowman point at him and laugh. Al Cochran, frowning, tried to pull Bowman away from the door, but Bowman entered, dragging Cochran behind him and talking loudly, "Come on, Big Al, let's have one on the rook!"

Cochran gloomily trailing behind, winced as Bowman banged Tommy on the back.

"Hey, rook! I hear you're celebrating. Don't you know you can't win the pennant on milk shakes! They're for kids!"

Tommy reached for his check and started to rise.

"Sit down," Bowman said roughly. "Have one on me."

"I don't want another one."

Bowman pushed Tommy back onto his stool. "When Buster buys, everybody drinks."

"Bring us some coffee," Cochran ordered.

Bowman drank his coffee, tossed a dollar bill on the counter and said, "I gotta finish my rounds for tonight, boys. See you in the headlines." He staggered through the door as Tommy stared after him.

"Why's he always getting on me, Al?"

"Don't worry about it, kid. Buster needles every rookie that comes up. Especially if he thinks they're any good."

Cochran sipped his coffee. "I'll tell you. When Bowman came up to the Bruins, they had a couple old-timers who treated him just like he treats you. Bowman was a real cocky kid from some small town in Pennsylvania. He couldn't take the needling, and they had a lot of fun with him. So he takes it out on everybody else. Don't let it get you down. It's all part of the game."

"One of these days I'm going to hit him right in the knee with a line drive!"

"Attaboy! Get 'em, Tiger!" Cochran pushed the empty coffee cup away and rose from the stool, stretching his arms above his head. "Come on. Let's hit the sack. I'm in there tomorrow."

The Bruins always drew well on weekends. Thomson Field was sold out for the Sunday game. Buster Bowman was to make his first start of the spring.

Thirty minutes before the game, Al Cochran was struck in the face by a wild throw as he warmed up in front of the dugout.

"See, rook. You learn something everyday," Bowman said to Tommy on the Bruins' bench. "Keep your eye on the ball—like Big Al!"

The joke was a poor one. Cochran's nose was broken. Tommy replaced him in right field.

For the first time Tommy could feel the tension of a large crowd watching a big-league ball game. His face already beaded with cold sweat, he stood on shaky legs as Bowman made the first pitch of the game. The batter blooped a short fly ball to right.

"You gotta come in!" yelled the Bruin second baseman. Tommy had hesitated momentarily, then charged after the ball. With a last-second lunge he speared it in the webbing of his glove.

The crowd applauded the catch. Tommy knew it should have been a routine play, but the roar of the fans was a bracing tonic. The short hairs rising on his neck relaxed. What could have been embarrassing turned out in his favor. The breaks of the game seemed to be going his way for a change.

Leading off the Bruins' half of the inning, he pushed a bunt toward third and beat the throw to first by half a step.

"Attaboy, kid," said Long John Mackey, the first-base coach. "Pick 'em up. Lay 'em down. Don't get picked off now."

Tommy could do no wrong this day. In the seventh

inning he hit a hanging curve ball over the right-field fence.

"Durned if the rook didn't look like he knew what was coming!" Mackey told reporters after the game. "I'll teach him the tricks yet!"

In the barrack Al Cochran lay on his bunk, his face half covered with bandage and tape, his right eye swollen black and blue.

"It may not look like it," he said to Tommy, "but this broken nose might be a good break. I won't be able to eat for a week!"

While Cochran's nose healed and his waistline shrank, Tommy James played right field for the Bruins. His despair of making it as a pro turned to dreams of big-league glory.

Long John Mackey, chewing and spitting tobacco, coached him in daily lessons on how to hit a curve ball. Tommy, awkward but willing, blistered his hands in extra practice.

"Get a golf glove for that right hand," Mackey advised him. "Hittin' the curve ball is no different than hittin' any other pitch. Lotta batters swing too soon. They can't judge the spin on the ball. They can't wait on it. The more curves you see, the more confidence you'll get, of course. When the pitch breaks into you, pull it. When it breaks away, hit it to the opposite field."

Tommy batted .326 for 10 games. His hot bat, speed and fresh spirit impressed Giff Browne.

"James is a great prospect," Browne said to one reporter. "But he's young and makes mistakes. He overthrows the cutoff on relays from the outfield, and he's kinda wild running the bases. Don't get me wrong. I like his speed. But we miss Cochran's power. Al's the only real long-ball threat on the club."

Cochran spent less and less time with Tommy. He and Buster Bowman ate many evening meals at the Ponce de Leon and seldom returned to the barrack until curfew.

Ten days before the regular season opened, the Bruins broke camp, leaving St. Augustine by train to start the exhibition road trip north. The veteran players groaned, complaining already about the long travel grind. Tommy, too young to know that too much travel can get boring, looked forward to the new towns, different ball parks, the big crowds at each game.

The Bruins lived on the train. Their special Pullman cars were parked on railroad sidings in each town while they played the daily games.

Bowman and Cochran played gin rummy for hours. Their card game was to last all season long, Bowman keeping a running score in a pad that fitted into a flap attached to his leather card case. Gleefully or grumblingly, according to his luck, he added up the results of the day's game each night. Since each played equally well, the loss or gain at the end of the season wouldn't amount to much.

"You play cards, rook?" Bowman asked Tommy one evening as the train pulled out of Richmond.

"No, Buster, I don't."

"Don't call me Buster, rook. It's still Mr. Bowman to you."

Cochran held up is hand as if to call time.

"Let's teach the kid how to play gin. Then if one of us breaks a leg and can't make a road trip during the season, Tommy can fill in." Cochran winked at Bowman, who grinned.

"Big Al, you're a thinkin' man. Yes, you are. Thinkin' all the time. OK, rook, sit down, put that big brown wallet on the table, and me an' Al will teach you how to play the game."

Tommy hesitated, but Cochran reached out to pull him into the compartment.

"Sit by me, kid. Gin rummy is a simple game, and you're a real fast learner accordin' to what I read in the paper. Anyway, we play small stakes—penny a point. Giff don't allow any big-money card games on this club."

"Hundred points is game, rook," said Bowman. Most you lose is a buck, right?"

By midnight Tommy had lost most of the games. Gin rummy is a simple game, but experience usually beats beginner's luck in card games.

At last Tommy threw down his hand and the money he owed. He walked angrily to the other end of the car, lay down in his roomette and stared at the ceiling light.

"Shoulda busted Bowman right in the teeth!" he mumbled. "Thinks I'm a hick." He pulled off his tie, unbuttoned his shirt.

"Cochran, too. Can't trust anybody in this game. Calls himself a friend. Just 'cause I take his job, he sucks me into a trap. I'll show 'em both. I know the big town better than both of 'em."

HOMETOWN BOY MAKES GOOD. Tommy could see the headlines. His mother had sent him clippings about every game he played. But he heard nothing from his father.

"Your father's bailiff is already a Tommy James fan!" she wrote.

In the compartment where they'd played cards, Cochran said to Bowman as he folded the table for the night, "We were a little rough on the kid."

"Tough. Let him learn the hard way. You and I did when we broke in."

"Understand Giff's cutting three guys before we open up. Gotta get down to 28 players."

"Forget it, big man. You won't be one of 'em! How's your ugly face?"

"Feels great. Bring on the photographers!"

The final exhibition game, in Baltimore, was rained out. Giff Bowman told the sportswriters that he hadn't made up his mind on the starting lineup for opening day.

"Buster will start for us, of course. If Adams pitches for them, I'll use Cochran in right field. Big Al always hits Adams well."

He didn't mention Tommy James.

The next morning in their own ball park the Bruins held their last preseason workout. Heavy dark clouds hung low, driving the dampness into suntanned faces that looked out of place in the wintry outdoors. The weatherman had promised fair skies for opening day, but for the moment Giff Browne was satisfied with an hour's batting practice and a short infield drill.

"Hey, kid!" Cochran said, running up the clubhouse steps behind Tommy. "Come on over to my locker with me."

Cochran took down what looked like a shrunken, sleeveless turtleneck sweater from a hanger in his locker. He handed it to Tommy.

"This is called a dickey. You put it on over your sweat shirt if it's cold. Keeps the neck warm."

When Tommy hesitated, Cochran insisted, "Go on, take it. I got another one. Listen, Tommy, I'm sorry about the other night. But you learned something, didn't ya? Never play cards for money. At least not with a coupla sharpies like me and Buster!"

Cochran laughed, but Tommy shrugged his shoulders and said nothing.

The clubhouse man tapped Tommy on the shoulder. "James, Giff wants to talk with you."

"OK," Tommy said. He could hardly keep the swagger from his stride as he walked to the manager's office in the front of the clubhouse. He could already hear Browne saying, "Kid, you're starting tomorrow. Get a good night's sleep." Or something like that.

Browne frowned at a paper on his desk as Tommy entered.

"Sit down, Tom." Browne sucked on the end of a

fountain pen. "I don't like to do this. No manager does. But we've decided to send you to Buffalo."

His voice seemed to fade away. Tommy leaned jerkily forward.

". . . good spring," Browne was saying. "You're gonna be a big-league ballplayer. I know that, and I want you to know I know it. But Cochran's ready to play now. All you'd do is sit on the bench if you stayed up here. You like to play ball, don't you?"

Tommy grinned weakly.

"OK. You go down there—that's our number-one farm club—and have a good season. You'll be back in no time."

Browne handed Tommy the pen, told him where to sign the assignment paper and held out his hand.

"Good luck, son."

Tommy's right hand was like a wet glove. He could barely feel the manager's reassuring grip. Fighting nausea, he left the room, walked out of the clubhouse and went home.

Mrs. James was talking on the telephone when Tommy walked into the house.

"Yes, We're *very* proud of him. The judge didn't like it when he went away this spring. But this is what Tommy wanted. He's grown up, you know. We're looking forward to opening day."

Tommy slipped quietly into his room. Why blame the whole thing on the judge! His mother had been so upset when he left she didn't even say good-bye!

Tommy sat on the edge of his bed. His old room seemed familiar, but he had forgotten it was so small.

All that junk they write about you in the papers doesn't mean a thing, he thought. *They say what you do right, but all the manager remembers is what you do wrong.*

HOMETOWN BOY MAKES GOOD makes great reading but it doesn't make you a pro.

"It isn't fair!" he yelled at himself in the mirror.

His tanned, unsmiling face looked back at him and didn't believe a word of it.

Mrs. James, by now a red-hot baseball fan, bubbled over at the supper table. She told him not to be nervous about starting opening day.

"It's just another ball game."

The judge, who had seen a late sports news item, sat quietly at the head of the table.

"I'm not starting tomorrow," Tommy said. "I'm not playing at all. They're sending me to the minors."

He sliced a forkful of steak with a steady hand.

"Oh!" Mrs. James cried, her face a mask of disbelief. "How can they do that to you! That's terrible! After you did so beautifully all spring! Well, you just tell them you won't go!"

"I'm all packed," Tommy said firmly. "I leave tomorrow."

"You will not!" Mrs. James said. "You'll do as we say. . . . Tell him, judge. Won't he ever learn anything?"

The judge chewed and swallowed a piece of meat,

cleared his throat, and said, "I thought he was wrong to go in the first place."

He picked up his knife, carved another slice and said, "And I think he would be wrong *not* to go now."

Judge James smiled at Tommy. The tone of his voice had a man-to-man pitch. "I think we've all learned something this spring. There will be another opening day. What is it they say?—'Wait till next year!'"

Shortstop

Bill Gutman

Dave Martin took four quick steps to his right, fielded the ball in the third-base hole, and in a smooth, graceful motion, fired it toward first. It was the way shortstops were supposed to make that play—clean and fast.

The first baseman on the Elmwood High School baseball team started his stretch—hesitated—then backed up. The ball hit in the dirt and skipped on past him.

"Come on, Anderson," Dave Martin shouted. "Make up your mind on those. You could have gloved it with a stretch. You do that in a real game and you make both of us look bad."

It was only the second day of practice for the Elmwood Rockets, but it was already evident that in senior transfer Dave Martin, the Rockets had a gem of a ballplayer. But the trouble was that they also had acquired a potential problem.

Martin had come to Elmwood from Rogers High. It was there that the 6-3, 180-pounder had earned All-State honors as a junior, batting .431 and playing his shortstop position with the facility of a Marty Marion— the great St. Louis shortstop in the days when the Cardinals dominated the National League.

After two years as the star of a very classy Rogers High team, Dave already had been approached by several scouts and was assured that another outstanding season was all he needed to receive a big bonus offer. Then he got the bad news. His father was being transferred and his new job was in the southern part of the state. It meant moving and going to a new school.

All Dave knew about Elmwood High was that it was located somewhere downstate and its baseball team had never made it past the first round of the big state tournament. When he arrived there, the first thing he did was look up baseball coach Glen Parker. He found the coach standing in the athletic office, took one look at his thin, 5-7 frame, and thought to himself: *This guy's no ballplayer.*

"Coach, I'm Dave Martin."

Parker turned and looked at the dark-haired, handsome youngster.

"Glad to meet you, Dave," he said, extending his hand. "I've already heard quite a bit about you. Happy to have you here."

"Thanks, Coach. To tell you the truth, I was looking forward to my last year at Rogers. We had a tremendous team with a great shot at the state title. And I had a fine chance of getting a pro contract this year."

"You still do. It shouldn't be any different for you at Elmwood."

"Your club won only five games last season. Do things look any better?"

"I don't know, Dave. The school lost its coach two years ago and I volunteered to be interim coach. I guess the program's suffered a bit. This year there are a lot of inexperienced kids coming out and I won't know any more until we start practicing in the spring."

"You mean there's no fall practice? The weather's great this time of year."

"Sorry, Dave. School rules. The baseball players are busy all spring and we try to give them time to study in the fall."

"Well, I'll need some equipment. I usually work out at least three times a week right through the winter. Is that against school rules, too?" Dave sounded annoyed.

"No, of course not. In fact, I'll give you a team roster. Maybe you can get some of the other guys to join you. It might be a good idea."

"That's not necessary, Coach. I'd prefer to work alone."

Martin wasn't kidding. His entire training program was mapped out. While everyone at Elmwood High concentrated on football, the solitary figure of Dave Martin was easily identifiable—baseball uniform and all—jogging, exercising, sometimes playing pepper games with other students. He didn't make any real friends.

It became increasingly obvious that baseball was the only thing on Dave's mind. And when it finally came time for practice to start, he was the first one out there, greeting each of his new teammates with an enthusiasm that had been missing in his relationships up to now. Baseball really turned him on.

"OK, let's go," he shouted as they came out of the gym one by one. "It's time for us to work. The winter's over. Get the lead out. We're gonna have a ball club here. A winning season. Let's want it. Let's work."

But Martin's enthusiasm lasted only as long as the first drill. He took one look at the ragtag collection trying out for the team and his heart sank. There were just three other seniors and it was doubtful whether any of them would start. The juniors and sophs were just beginners. Martin couldn't see how Elmwood would even field a respectable team, much less hope for any kind of season.

And the following days of practice only showed the degree of ineptitude that plagued the Rockets. Coach Parker tried to bring his club together, but although he taught the fundamentals well, he lacked the intuitive feel for the game that a successful coach must have. And a look at the starting lineup only served to stoke Dave Martin's worst fears.

At first base was junior Carl Anderson, slow and inexperienced, with little knowledge of the split-second footwork needed around the bag. He had some potential as a hitter, but that was all. Little Doug Gannett, another junior, played second. He could go to his left, but not his right, he made the double-play pivot like a man skidding on a banana peel. At third was senior Barry

Thomas. He was the captain of the team, so Coach Parker felt he should be playing somewhere.

The outfield consisted of two juniors and a sophomore, and only Bill Nevin in center inspired any confidence. A fly ball to Andy Cornwall or Bert Jackson was an adventure. But Nevin couldn't hit a lick; the other two looked as if they could be hitters, with practice.

Russ Gammon was the catcher. Most of his throws to second came in on a bounce. The pitching staff consisted of a senior, a junior, and a sophomore. One couldn't throw a ball through a cobweb; the other two couldn't find home plate.

Only about 40 fans braved the cold, windy, spring weather as Elmwood opened its season against the Engineers of Clinton High. In the Clinton half of the first, there was a sharp grounder up the middle. Martin darted behind the bag, scooped it up, and rifled his throw to first. The ball came in shoulder high—and tore right through the webbing of Anderson's glove. Safe! And an error on the first baseman.

"Take it easy on those throws, Dave," shouted Parker from the bench.

The next batter hit a routine bouncer to short. Martin fielded it and started going to second. Then he stopped. No one was there. Gannett forgot to cover.

"Wake up, Doug," Dave said. "Do I have to do it all by myself?"

Two hits and another error followed before Martin made a leaping grab of a liner to end the inning. Clinton held a 3-0 lead.

Martin was first up in the second. Clinton had a big right-hander on the mound and the count went to 2-1 before Dave slammed a liner into the left centerfield gap for a double. But he stayed on second as Thomas and Cornwall fanned, and Gammon grounded to second.

The first two innings set the pattern as Clinton went on to win, 9-2. Martin drove in the first Elmwood run with a triple and scored the second on a ground out. He had three hits on the day and made several nifty stops in the field. But it didn't take him long to realize that he had to ease up on his tosses to first. Anderson simply couldn't handle his bullet throws. And if there was one thing Dave Martin liked to do, it was gun that baseball across the diamond.

"OK, fellas, don't feel too bad," said Parker after the game. "It was the first one for a lot of you. We made mistakes, but that's to be expected. You've got to practice the fundamentals so you know what to do out there—when to cover a base, where to throw, how to play the hitters. I think we're gonna improve and win some ball games real soon. What do you say?"

The entire team shouted a rallying "YEAH!"—all except Dave Martin. He knew what he had to do. That night he'd write every scout who had seen him play last year. He'd make sure they saw him again. Even at Elmwood.

Three games and three losses later, a man approached Dave as he came out on the field for his warm-ups.

"Hello, Dave."

It was "Digger" Cabelli, a scout for the Giants who had been following him for two years.

"Am I glad to see you, Digger," Dave said. "Did you get my letter?"

"Sure did, kid. The guys at Rogers told me you were down here, so I wired another scout to pick you up. But I guess he didn't follow up on the lead. When I got your letter last week, I figured I'd better call in person. How's the ball club?"

"Awful, Digger, just terrible. Most of these kids can't get out of their own way."

"How about you? Improved any from last year?"

"I think so, but I'm having a tough time showing it at this place."

"Hey, you better show something. I can't recommend a kid on what he did last year. But I'm not worried. I think you've got what it takes. See you after the game."

With Cabelli in the stands, Martin was psyched up for the first time all year. He fielded a routine grounder in the first and unleashed a cannonball toward first. Needless to say, it whizzed right past the startled Anderson and the official scorer called it an error on the throw.

"Come on, Anderson. Wake up over there," Dave yelled. "You can't play patty-cake baseball all your life."

"Take it easy, Dave," Parker shouted from the bench.

In the fourth, an opposing player hit a slow grounder toward third. Both Thomas and Martin charged it. The third baseman was set for the pickup when Martin reached in front of him, barehanded the ball, and made an off-balance throw to first. Anderson gloved it for the out and the fans cheered the play. As Dave returned to his position, Thomas walked toward him.

"That was my ball. You made me look like a jerk cutting in front of me that way. Let me go after those from now on."

"Listen, there's some new rules around here," Dave shot back. "Anything I can reach, I field. You couldn't have made that throw to first. Be smart about it, huh?"

Then in the fifth, Martin poled one over the left-fielder's head and legged out his first homer of the year, a 400-foot shot that brought a broad smile to Digger Cabelli's face. It didn't matter that hardly any of his teammates congratulated him. He felt good.

But the feeling was short-lived. With a man on first in the sixth, the batter hit a grounder to Gannett at second. Dave cut over to cover the bag. He timed it just right— so he thought. But Gannett couldn't get the ball out of his mitt. He finally did and threw it toward second, the ball arriving at the same time as the sliding baserunner, who slammed into Martin, knocking him down. The ball squirted loose and both runners were safe. Dave had taken a good crack in the shin and was enraged.

"What's the matter with you, Gannett?" he cried. "You got butter for hands, or you just trying to get me killed?"

"You'll never know," mumbled the second baseman as he walked back to position.

Dave was robbed of a hit in the seventh, but made a

great grab of a liner in the eighth. It didn't help. Elmwood lost another one, 7-1.

After the game, he sought out Cabelli. He found the old scout talking to Parker, waited for the coach to leave, then approached him.

"See what I'm up against, Digger? This place is too much."

"I see a lot of things, kid. You shouldn't be so rough on those other guys. They can't help what they are out there. And you've got that coach of yours pretty upset about it all."

"That guy! I don't think he ever played the game. Coach Yates had it all over him."

"Maybe he did. And maybe you were with a winner at Rogers and a loser here. But a ballplayer makes the best of bad situations. It won't last forever."

"I'm trying, Digger. But if I'm not careful, one of those guys will get me killed."

Cabelli laughed. "Yeah, you really took a tumble out there. Just keep playing your game, Dave. I still think you've got what it takes. But a little advice from a guy who's been around awhile—play *with* those guys, tough as it may be. Don't keep bucking them. I'll be seeing you before the year is out. Good luck."

As Martin went back to the locker room, Glen Parker stopped him. "Look, Dave," he said, "you told me the first time we met that you weren't happy being here. OK—I didn't make a trade with Rogers to get you. Sure, I was happy about it. I was getting a major-league prospect, someone I thought would help the boys become better ballplayers, help the team win a few games. Instead, what did I get? A moody egotist, who can't accept the fact that he's not playing with world champions."

"I'm sorry if that's the way it is," Martin answered, "but baseball is more than a fun game to me. For 10 years now, I've been working for one thing—to be a big-league ballplayer. And I can't let a bunch of patsies ruin it for me."

"But you're only 17. You've got plenty of time. I'm sure you'll pretty much have your pick of colleges—"

"College! I don't want to go to college. I want to sign now and start playing next year."

"Isn't your education important to you?"

"What do I have to study English, math, and history for? The only history I'm interested in is the history of baseball. I have no desire to waste my time at some college. That's why this year is so important."

"Are you sure?" Parker asked.

"Absolutely."

"Then there's nothing more I can say."

Three days later, the Rockets took the field against Carterville, a small high school in a nearby town with a team traditionally the weakest in the county. The game was a comedy of errors, Elmwood winning, 8–6, for its first victory of the year. All Dave Martin did was slam three doubles and a homer, steal two bases, and make several sparkling plays in the field. His batting average was up to .553 and that offered him a small measure of consolation. He was feeling good, and maybe that's why he approached Carl Anderson in the locker room.

"Hey, Carl, I'd like to talk to you for a minute."

The first baseman was startled. He didn't feel like hearing more criticism from Martin.

"What is it?" he asked curtly.

"I've been watching you, the way you play the bag. Your big problem is your feet. You're so busy thinking how to shift them, that you're losing the ball. You've got to commit with your feet first, then concentrate on making the rest of the play. Here, let me show you what I mean."

Dave looked around, then grabbed an empty equipment bag from the corner of the room. He folded it to about the size of a base and dropped it on the floor in front of Anderson, who was sitting open-mouthed, staring at his teammate.

"Now look. As soon as a ball is hit to any of us, you move to the bag and plant yourself squarely in front of it, facing directly at the man who's making the play. Then keep your eye on the ball. As soon as he releases it, you've got to commit. You've got to judge whether the throw is going to come to the right or left, be high or low. Then once your feet are set, you can concentrate on catching the ball. (Dave demonstrated with some nifty footwork, jumping to the bag several different ways, from all sides.) That's why you have so much trouble with me. I throw hard. You're usually still playing with your feet when the ball gets there. Otherwise you'd catch it."

Dave turned and picked up the bag. He started to bring it back when Anderson finally spoke.

"Dave, do you think we could stay after practice tomorrow and work on it for awhile?"

"Well, I don't—why not? I've got the time."

The next day they recruited one of the sophomores to hit grounders and Dave started firing throws at Anderson, easy at first, then with increasing velocity. After each toss, he told the first baseman what he was doing wrong and had him try it several times without a throw. By the end of the two-hour session, Anderson was showing marked improvement. And his confidence was growing steadily.

"I think I'm getting the hang of this now, Dave," he said. "No one's ever shown me some of these things or taken the time to work on them like this. I really appreciate it. Maybe pretty soon you can cut a few loose during a game and not have to worry."

"I hope so. Just keep going over your moves. Before you know it, that bag will be a part of you. You'll know exactly where it is at all times."

Two days later, the lessons paid off. Anderson made only one error all afternoon, and Elmwood came close, losing to a good Bancroft team, 4–2. Dave collected just one hit, a third-inning double, but he didn't have the usual feeling of disgust as he prepared to shower. He didn't know why—until he saw Carl Anderson come in.

"Hey, Carl, you played a great game out there today," he heard himself saying. "Next time we'll get 'em."

"Thanks, Dave. I felt better. Now I'm only half scared when I see you crank up that arm of yours."

Both boys laughed. It was the first time since the season started that there was no noticeable tension in the air. Coach Parker liked that, but said nothing. He didn't want to chance upsetting the delicate balance that was holding his team together.

By the next practice, the word was out. First it was third baseman Thomas. He simply approached Martin and said, "Dave, help."

The two stayed late. Dave showed him how to be always in position to move toward first, even on simple pickups, so he'd be in better throwing range and could get more on the ball. He explained how it was easier for a shortstop to take a pop behind third, and told Thomas when to throw sidearm and when to stand up and gun overhand. He made him get down lower on the ball and field more aggressively.

"Remember," he said, "I've got more range than you. So play tight to the line. That'll eliminate the backhand play most times and I'll cover you in the hole. And let's talk to each other out there."

"Sure, Dave. You're the boss," said Thomas.

With Gannett, it was more than a matter of positioning. The little second baseman simply didn't have the arm to make a strong throw to first on the double play, even after he perfected the art of pivoting. Whenever possible, Martin said he'd run to the bag and throw to first himself on the DP attempt. If he was going the other way, he told Gannett to make sure of the out at second and not worry about a relay to first. "We'll get by without it."

But he was able to give Gannett some of the other basics of his position. He had him always playing a step or two to the right of the normal position to cut down the chances of a backhand play. He showed him the art of backpedaling and made sure that Anderson would work with Gannett verbally. Almost without knowing it, Dave Martin had become the infield coach—and he was liking it.

It didn't take long to produce results—a 4–3 win over Calvert, a 6–4 victory against Morgantown, and a 3–1 upset triumph against Boulder City. Now the Rockets were meeting Devon High in what was termed the "biggest game of the year."

"This is a solid team, no real weaknesses," Parker told his club before the game. "We have to play perfect baseball to win. Let's give 'em a game."

During warm-ups, Dave spotted a pair of grizzled old-timers in the stands, talking to each other and making notes on their respective clipboards. Scouts!

Wow! he thought. *I've got to put on a show today. They're probably here to look at some Devon guys. It's up to me to turn it around—fast.*

There were two out when Dave stepped to the plate in the top of the first. He was a menacing right-handed batter with a slightly closed stance, bat held high over his head.

"Hiya, star," said the burly Devon catcher. "Heard all

about you being a hotshot. Why don't you show us something?"

"Don't worry, Fats," Dave answered. "I won't disappoint you."

On the second pitch he bunted down the first-base line, taking the Devon club by surprise. He sped toward first, thinking about stealing second—when the ball cracked into the first baseman's mitt.

"Out!" cried the ump, jerking his thumb into the air.

A surprised Martin trotted slowly back toward the bench. As he passed home plate, the big catcher smiled.

"A little gift from 'Fats,' hotshot," he said.

When the catcher came up in the second, Dave dug in. Sure enough, he hit a high bouncer up the middle. Dave charged quickly to his left, gloved the ball behind the bag, and fired hard toward first. The ball was low and Anderson couldn't handle it, the catcher winding up with a big smile at second base, and Dave was tagged with the error.

Martin looked at his first baseman, who was standing there, head down. "OK, Carl, you made the right move for it. Just one of those things. Settle down." Anderson smiled slightly, but Dave was looking back up at the scouts, who were busily writing.

In the fourth, Martin singled—and was promptly thrown out trying to steal second. He glanced at the scouts again. By now he must have been just another ballplayer to them. And he had to hand it to that catcher; he sure had a great arm.

To this point, the Rockets had been holding the Devon Dragons in check. But in the fifth, the home club broke it open. It started with a single. The next batter hit a grounder to Martin, and Gannett promptly dropped the throw at second. Then there was a pop to short left. Martin backpedaled, called for the ball, and was ready to run it to the infield when left-fielder Cornwall slammed into him. The ball dropped to the ground and the sacks were loaded. A stinging double to right center cleared the bases.

That did it. Dave doubled home a run in the sixth and Cornwall two more in the eighth, but Devon coasted home with a 7–3 win. After the game, Dave saw the two scouts talking with several of the Devon players, including the high-powered catcher, but no one approached him. He felt as if it were the end.

"Sorry, Dave. We had a bad day." Carl Anderson was talking and some of the others were with him. Dave had been sitting by himself in the locker room, his head buried in his hands. Now he looked up.

"It's OK, fellas. Plenty of season left yet. We'll bounce back."

Maybe. But Dave wondered if *he* could bounce back. There was no way to build a reputation at Elmwood. Just not enough time and not enough ballplayers to support him. He felt as if his two years at Rogers had been wasted.

"No, it's not OK," Barry Thomas said. "We went to pieces out there today and we didn't like it. We're going to need your help again. How about it?"

"You've got it. Why not?" he said. But it didn't take away all of the pain.

In the ensuing weeks, Dave worked with the team. Though no one said it, the big shortstop was obviously a better teacher than Parker, whose own playing experience was limited, and who lacked practical knowledge of the game. He did his best with the boys, but it was Dave Martin who was slowly getting through to them.

He showed the outfielders where to play the hitters, how to go after a ball. During games he shouted instructions to everyone, keeping them aware of the situations, telling them where to throw if the ball came to them. On the bench, he sat alongside Parker and made suggestions on bunting, stealing, hit-and-run plays, the whole range of heads-up baseball. He worked with the team on the art of hitting, adjusting batting stances, telling players how much to choke up, making many of them cut down on their swings. And through it all, his own game improved. He didn't have to hold back any more in fear that his teammates couldn't handle his throws, or would be in his way.

And the team followed his lead, playing two games over .500 the rest of the way and finishing only three games under the break-even mark. Dave won three games with clutch hits, and even saved one with a ninth-inning relief job on the mound, something he once vowed never to do, for fear of hurting his arm. He was enjoying baseball again, and in a different sort of way, maybe enjoying it more than ever before.

Despite the club's under .500 record, they would still

be competing in the state tournament. Every team had a chance to make it through the playdowns. Elmwood was scheduled to meet Jefferson, an above-average club, in the first round. Before the game, Dave Martin had a visit from an old friend.

"Hello, Dave," Digger Cabelli said. "I see you boys have been winning a few."

"Hi, Digger. Yeah, we've come on a bit. I didn't think I'd be seeing you again."

"Hey, kid. A ballplayer's a ballplayer, no matter where he's operating. Now listen. I've got my boss with me today. Just play your usual game and I think we can talk turkey with you."

Dave's eyes lit up. He felt a twinge of nervous excitement shoot through his body.

"OK, Digger. Thanks for the tip. I'll try not to let you down."

Cabelli smiled, smacked Martin on the rump, and returned to his seat.

Once on the field, Dave sensed the butterflies in his stomach, a feeling he hadn't known since his first varsity game, as a sophomore. *I'll be all right as soon as they hit one to me,* he thought.

He got his wish as the second Jefferson batter slammed a grass-cutter right at him. He went down to field it and came up with a handful of air. The ball had stayed low and scooted through his legs into left field. He glanced quickly in the direction of Cabelli.

"Calm down, Dave." It was Thomas, the third baseman. "Just play your game. We're all pulling for you."

The next batter hit a high hopper his way. He grabbed it, flipped to second and waited for the disaster. But Gannett pivoted perfectly and fired a strike to Anderson for the double play.

Martin was batting in the cleanup spot. With two out, Cornwall slammed a double to left and Dave came up with a chance to drive in a run. Jefferson had a big fast-baller on the mound, the kind of pitcher Martin could eat up.

The first two pitches were wide. *He'll have to come in with the fast one now,* he said to himself, digging in. But the right-hander curved him, and Dave was out in front, lifting a harmless pop to third to end the inning. He looked bad on it.

When the next grounder came his way, he figured he'd have to show off his arm, no matter what the result at the other end. So he uncorked a bullet. It didn't feel right leaving his hand and he saw it heading for the dust about two feet in front of Anderson. Dave Martin actually had his eyes closed when he heard the roar of the crowd and the umpire holler, "Out!" It was one of the few times all year that Anderson had made the scoop.

The next time the first baseman didn't have the same chance. Martin's throw sailed about four feet over his head, allowing two Jefferson runs to score. Dave could see Cabelli talking heatedly with the man next to him. He felt everything slipping away. He had to do some-thing fast.

In the sixth, he ripped a single to left, rounded first and headed to second. He was thrown out by a good three feet.

"What's the matter, Dave?" asked Parker. "You're too smart for a bonehead play like that."

"I had to try it," was the panicky answer.

With two out in the seventh, a walk, single, and walk loaded the bases for Jefferson. The next batter worked the count to 2–2, then lofted a high pop to short left. Dave started back, turned, lost the ball, turned back and finally got under it. But his feet tangled and he started to go down, the ball glancing off the top of his glove. He pictured all three runs coming in and didn't even want to look—until the ump shouted "Out!" once more.

Dave turned around to see Andy Cornwall clutching the ball. Cornwall had been right behind him and grabbed the ball as it came off Dave's glove. Elmwood was out of another jam.

With Jefferson leading by 2–0 in the eighth, Gannett and Cornwall singled. Now Dave had a shot at driving in the tying runs. He dug in against the Jefferson hurler.

The first pitch was down the pipe and he took it for a strike. He guessed fast ball on the next, timed it, and swung from the heels. Another towering pop-up, this one to second. A base hit by Gammon brought in one run, but Thomas fanned to end the inning.

With two down in the Jefferson ninth, the batter hit a shot into the hole. Dave moved laterally after the ball, backhanded it, stopped, and fired a cannon to first, nipping the runner by a stride. It was a brilliant play, but the last one Dave Martin would make for Elmwood High

School. He trotted off the field, head down, then sat on the bench as the Rockets went out in order and wound up on the short end of a 2−1 score.

One or two players patted Dave on the back when it was over, but most left him alone. Parker quietly congratulated his young team and told them they'd have more confidence next season. Then he sought out his erstwhile star and found him sitting alone in an empty office adjoining the dressing room.

"Your first bad game of the year, Dave. Sorry it had to happen today."

"The guys really came through," Dave said quietly. "And I lost it. I lost everything."

"Hey," said Parker, putting his hand on the youngster's shoulder. "Do you think it would have been that close if it weren't for you? You made ballplayers out of them. Two months ago Jefferson would have buried us. There'll be other days, a lot of them for you. Everyone knows how talented you are."

"But I choked it, Coach. Thank the guys for me anyway. I can't face them now."

"You will later. And you didn't choke anything. Now there's someone to see you."

Parker left and Digger Cabelli entered, sitting down alongside Dave, who looked sadly into the deeply lined face of his friend.

"I guess you know the verdict," he said. "The one day they came over. Tough luck. But I'm not giving up. I'll have them back again. It's only a matter of time."

"Back where?" Dave said. "The season's over."

"There's always next year. You're just a kid. Another year or two will be to your advantage, believe me."

Dave didn't answer. He had no answer. He wanted Cabelli to tell him what he already knew, what he had known for a long time.

"I talked to the head men at Arizona State and Southern Cal. They're both interested. And I know a couple of others. You'll be hearing from them next week. Don't let the opportunity pass by."

With that, Cabelli touched him lightly on the shoulder and left.

The shortstop just sat there. *Maybe it wasn't all over,* he thought. *Maybe better days lay ahead.* Deep down inside, he knew it. His future was still exciting, maybe more so than before, though he didn't know exactly why. Anyway, he was going to take another look at the college thing.

Seconds later, Thomas and Anderson poked their heads through the door.

"Dave," Anderson said, "We're all having a party at my house tonight. We'd like you to come."

Dave looked at them, both smiling at him, not having to say any more. Now he knew—about a lot of things.

"I'll be there," he said.

The Game Ball

A. R. Swinnerton

D aryl didn't have red hair, he wasn't from Texas, and neither his first or last name suggested a nickname.

It seemed important to him at that time. A nickname meant acceptance, being part of the group, an affectionate title by his peers which would help break down his shyness.

In the dugout he sat quietly, in the midst of the banter around him but not part of it. At the far end of the bench, shouting out to his batter, the coach leaned forward thoughtfully, glancing down nervously toward his batting order.

"Knew it," he grumped. "Got him on that same pitch again. You're up, Hunnecutt. Get something started now. Come on!"

Daryl walked toward the plate, jockeying his helmet. Skip Bozart, the batter who had fanned, passed him with head down, failure written on his face clear as a scroll.

On the mound, staring at Daryl as if he were his blood enemy, the pitcher began the duel. At ease now, Daryl logged the first pitch. He could have reached it, but he held up. Back in Connecticut, where he had played before this summer, the pitching was faster, more consistent, yet he still hit well over .375.

Behind him, the bench was quiet. It always was when he batted. No "Come on, Daryl," no "Hang in there, buddy." What did he have to do to win them over?

Count 2–1, action time. The pitcher leaned forward, rotated the ball, took a full windup. The ball sailed in, high and tight. Daryl stepped back, waited a fraction of a second, then swung hard. There was no sound, no leathery crack. It was as if his bat intercepted the ball in flight, recoiled as it absorbed the shock, then flicked it outward like a stone from a sling.

The center fielder panicked, waving at the ball as it cleared his glove. Daryl pounded into third, breathing hard. His dugout stirred, nothing more. What did he have to do to get their endorsement—steal home?

It could be done. Worked maybe once or twice a season. The trick was to get the pitcher off guard. Stay chained to the bag, yawn a couple of times and hope the batter would hang in there long enough to set the trap.

Arms folded, he waited. After the first two tosses, he could see the pitcher was taking the bait. With two outs, why worry about that duck on third? Concentrate on the batter, that made sense.

Two wide ones, a strike, then a foul slice. The pitcher had his sign, contorted himself into his stretch. Daryl began walking, then with a wild yell, broke for the plate. The pitcher saw him, heard him yell, tried to change his delivery from breaking pitch to fast ball. It cost him the game.

The ball came in high, first base side. It hit the edge of the catcher's glove, trickled away. He scratched for it, lunged through the dust for some part of Daryl's anatomy, but he was late. "Safe!" bawled the umpire.

Daryl felt his knees shake. They usually did, after the action was over. The guys muttered, "Nice going," as if he tried but lost the game for them. By the time he'd gotten a drink and splashed some water over this face, he was alone in the empty dugout.

Save for Charlie Branch, their coach. He was a slightly paunchy man in his thirties, who walked with a limp. An ex-minor leaguer, Daryl figured, but no one knew for sure.

Charlie waited for him near the bleachers. "Nice game, Daryl," he offered. "Ride home?"

"Thanks," said Daryl, avoiding his eyes. "I've got my bike."

"Shove it in the back," said Charlie. "That's a long climb up the hill, without a shift on your bike."

Charlie swung the bike into the wide rear end of his station wagon, and they eased across the grass to the road. "I've watched you," said Charlie. "You've got natural talent and playing instinct. Everything comes easy for you."

Daryl stared straight ahead. "On the field, yeah."

The coach shifted into low at the bottom of the hill.

"Like this buggy," he said. "She's old, but she's got plenty of zip to go up without shifting. But I gear her down just so she don't get too big for her britches. Don't want anyone to say I'm hot-roddin'."

Daryl felt uneasy. The coach was trying to tell him something, but he wasn't sure what. He took a crack at it. "That's the only way I know how to play," he said. "All out, hard as I can."

Charlie nodded. "And you're right," he said. "Only thing you might not have thought of is that the other guys play the same way. With one difference."

Daryl waited as the car stopped in his driveway. "They're good guys, Daryl," said Charlie. "They play hard, from their spikes to that little button on top of their caps, but it's just a game. They'll never play pro ball, never see their name in the record books, never have fan clubs, never get bonuses or even waivers. Sure, they talk about it, dream about it. Then you came along with your hustle and talent, and you busted their dreams. You're going to be what they'll never be, and they know it."

Charlie helped him slide his bike from the wagon. "You mean they're jealous of me?" asked Daryl.

"More like envy, Daryl. But you give 'em time. You're a new boy, you showed 'em up on the field of honor. Just let 'em know you're human, and they'll come around. 'Bye."

If anything, his play improved. He could play shallow in center field, making outs of bloop singles, then race back for deep fly balls, stabbing everything as if he were a heat-seeking missle.

At bat, he was almost unstoppable. The ball seemed to float in for him, and he could call a better game than the ump. You could pitch to him or walk him, but you couldn't fool him.

In the dugout, the cone of silence got worse, the better he played. He understood it now, but that didn't help. Worse, even the coach avoided him, and even though Daryl understood why, it hurt. What must he do—strike out three times with the bases loaded before he'd be one of them? He'd be glad when the season was over.

The game Saturday afternoon was a big one. To stay in contention for the play-offs, they had to win. Charlie made some changes in his line-up, but their pitching was flabby, their infield erratic, and their best hitter outside of Daryl was Mayberry, their worst pitcher.

Every game, with few exceptions, takes on its own character, once play starts. This one followed a script of poor pitching, heavy hitting, infield outs turned generously into two-base errors, and simultaneous and copious sweating by both coaches.

They took the field in the last of the seventh with a shaky 10–9 lead. Daryl stationed himself close in, but the coach waved him back, even though Whitby was up. He was a pesky hitter, a guy who could find the holes, but who barely ever hit deep.

Two out, bases loaded. The catcher and shortstop

walked out to the mound. Daryl could see Charlie Branch squatting in front of the dugout, letting the three of them work it out. "Let's go!" shouted the umpire.

Working carefully and nervously, the pitcher coaxed a full count on Whitby. Daryl wanted to come in, but he stayed put. The pitcher stretched, glanced apprehensively at the runners leading off, then politely grooved one.

It hung over the plate as big as a croquet ball. Eyes lighting up, Whitby swung. Leaping off his bat, the ball was no sneaky grounder but a long, high shot just to Daryl's left. He judged it, ran back, eyes glued to the white speck. He had it, he knew he did.

Up about 50 feet, just as it completed its apogee, the ball caught the sun and seemed to split in two. It wavered, began dropping short. He dug towards it as it tumbled down a step ahead of him, and he lunged for it.

Made it. Made something. His glove felt light, there was no solid smack. Curled up in the pocket, staring up at him through dazed but malevolent eyes, was a pigeon. Horrified, he stared back at it, tried to grab it. With an angry squawk, it flew away, over the field. A roar went up from the stands.

Moss, the right fielder, picked up the ball, grinning from ear to ear. "It's all over, Daryl, and we lost, but you get the game ball for catching the game bird."

Red-faced, he walked in slowly, but his teammates ran out and mobbed him, pounding his back and mussing his hair. "Hey," someone yelled. "Hey, Birdie! That was some kind of big-league catch!"

The Game Ball

They were smiling at him, ribbing him, and the tension was gone. He had his nickname, had come by it honestly, and he was one of them. It was the start of the best summer of his life, and he would remember it a few years later when he was Birdie Hunnecutt, AL rookie of the year.

He'd always remember that summer.

Bunt

Mary Fantina

If Bunt Wiley had a real first name it was forgotten years and years before he got to the major leagues. Bunt played shortstop for the Panthers and had done so for 15 years. He was unquestionably the best. He led off for the Panthers and usually batted over .300 with 40 rbi's or so, but there was one problem—he bunted. He always bunted. Here was a man with 1,513 lifetime hits; 1,510 singles and three doubles. He doubled as a rookie when the third baseman for the Reds broke his leg as he charged the bunt and doubled again 10 years later when the Dodgers, angered by his 5 for 5 performance, moved both their shortstop and third baseman in past the mound and he lofted a bunt over their heads. The third time was against the Giants, early this season. With the tying run on third, Wiley had bunted down the line and sped to second as Bill Morrison, third baseman for the Giants, desperately and unsuccessfully waited for it to roll foul.

Bunt was a switch hitter, of course, because as his

critics said, there was no hitting ability in bunting. It was rumored that he was a natural right-handed hitter, had he ever tried. His stance looked like anyone's; he crouched, but not too much; he took practice swings—actual swings—but not too many; he had the bat cocked and ready on his shoulder. He had never, not once, swung away, not in the minor leagues and not in batting practice. And he had one other quality in the batter's box, he was quick and agile. He almost never was hit-by-pitch, but not for lack of trying by the opposing pitchers. And this season, for the first time ever, one of his teammates worked up the nerve to ask him why he always bunted.

The Panthers had a rookie centerfielder, Harry Webster, who was phenomenal. Webster was the cockiest guy on the team, but even he needed the whole team to goad him on to ask Bunt.

"C'mon, Harry, what are you waiting for?" said Dan Washington, catcher, as they were getting dressed for a game.

"Don't rush me," said Harry, trying again to get out of it. "What do *you* think, Terry?"

"Don't look at me, kid," said Terry D'Angelo, the team's first baseman, "I already know why he bunts."

"Why?" demanded Harry. He thought no one knew. There were snickers from all present; they had all, at one time or another, asked Terry's opinion on just this topic.

"He bunts," said Terry quite seriously, "because he wants to."

"Oh, brother!" said Harry disgusted.

"Well, ask the man," laughed Tim Starker, the left fielder, "if you really want to know."

"Well, he's not here," said Harry, "or I would do just that!"

"Who's not here?" asked Bunt as he and Ex Connors, both already in uniform, came in.

"Well, uh, I mean . . ." started Harry, but the laughs and giggles of the rest of the locker room gave him the necessary boldness.

"You," he said firmly. You could hear a pin drop. Bunt and Ex were mildly surprised, but Bunt waited politely. Harry was losing his nerve, but he was stuck.

"I was just wondering," asked Harry apologetically, "why you always bunt?"

"I have a reason," said Bunt easily, and he and Ex went out to the field.

"Well, what do you suppose that means?" asked Dan.

"Darned if I know," said Terry.

On the field, Bunt and Ex worked out. Extra Bases Connors used to be called Slugger. It was only natural, however, when Bunt joined the team that Slugger would be called Extra Bases because he hit for extra bases, since Bunt was called Bunt because he bunted. In Bunt's rookie year, this philosophy was immortalized in print, thusly: ". . . the Panthers' three runs were accounted for by bunts by Bunt Wiley coming in front of triples by Extra Bases Connors."

Ex was the right fielder for the Panthers and had been for 17 years. He had been all-star right fielder many times. At their home park, the short porch in right field jutted out drastically at the foul pole. In this area the fence was just over three feet high and only the hardiest and quickest individuals sat there. It was not unusual for the lumbering Connors to be seen diving in, both fair and foul, to match catches. He also entered these seats if he made the catch on the run nearby because he could rarely stop himself in time. The right field area was called Connors Corner for this reason, and because he hit most of his home runs there.

He was a big man like power hitters normally are, hitting about 35 home runs a year. He got singles too, but he almost never bunted because, for one thing, he wasn't good at it and for another, he was awfully slow.

Bunt and Ex were best friends and by virtue of both their seniority and their spirit, they were the team leaders—the heart and soul of the Panthers. The Panthers needed heart; they always finished second, except when they finished third. They could never catch the Giants— at least not in Ex's memory, and he'd been there the longest. It was their pitching, they all thought, that year after year made them second best. Everyone on the team could hit because Ex spent hours teaching them, and everyone on the team could bunt because Bunt showed them how. The only one who objected to these long hours of extra batting practice was Harry Webster. Harry was an instant star and didn't hold much with practicing— particularly bunting. Anyone can bunt, he thought, and chances are even it will be a good bunt.

"Look, Harry," said Bunt at practice one day, "no one on this team makes out when he bunts, except me, 'cause I always bunt. When anyone else has to bunt, it's important. He has to do it right."

"But I've been trying for hours!" objected Harry.

"Are you in this for the money, or the glory, or what?" demanded Bunt. Harry glared at him for a minute, then he took his bat back to the plate.

"It's not for the money," he mumbled to himself.

This year was different for the Panthers. They had George Lukas and Pablo Sakimoto. They were pitchers, and they were good. Pablo was a rookie from the Philippines and his specialty was control; George had been recently traded from the Yankees for the Panthers' centerfielder Bud Marshall, and his specialty was speed. Dan Washington said he couldn't see the ball when George pitched; he just caught it by putting his mitt up where he heard it whistling in.

With their new-found pitching, it was a race, a real race. With only a week left in the regular season, they were tied with the Giants. If they could beat the giants two out of three now, they'd win the pennant.

Game one started on a cloudy Sunday afternoon at the Giants' home stadium. George Lukas started against Seth Wendall. Of all people, thought Bunt, the Lunatic Lefty had to start against them. The Giants were known for throwing the brush back or actual beanball, anyway, and Seth, who held a 10-year grudge against Bunt for breaking up a perfect game once, didn't need any push to chase him out of the batter's box. So it was the case that Bunt never bunted well against Seth because he was always diving out of the box, or at least leaning away. He did reach first a lot against him, though.

Bunt studied Seth as he warmed up. He was in a nasty mood today, all right. More Panthers than just Bunt would be jumping out of the way. Bunt was right; through six innings there had been two hit batsmen. Ex was very nearly hit in the head. It was only through uncommon quickness that he escaped injury. The normally calm and peaceable Ex picked himself up and took his bat as he proceeded a few steps toward the defiant pitcher. The Giant players came to the edge of the dugout, poised and ready. The Panthers were ready, too.

"Lefty," he said in a calm voice, "don't do that again," and with that he spread his hands apart on the bat and ripped it in half. Seth nearly swallowed his gum and the Giants slunk back to their seats. Ex didn't get any more inside pitches. For the rest of the game, they all missed low and away.

Big George, on the other hand, had the Giant hitters talking to themselves. They had only one hit, and a bunt at that. But in the sixth, George led off with a double— only his third hit of the year. Bunt followed George in the order, and it was a sure bet he would bunt. Coach Adams frowned as Bunt approached the plate; there was after all, something to be said for the element of surprise. The Giants put on the exaggerated Wiley shift. All the infielders moved in for the bunt. Bunt grinned to himself. This was the wrong shift to use with a man on second.

While George stood on the base watching Scotty Batch give the signs at third, Bunt stepped up to the plate. George took his lead. It was a big one for a pitcher, and Seth warmed up. George's lead got bigger and he began to run. The infield came alive with activity. Harrelson in left broke for third and so did third baseman Morrison. As Morrison left his spot, Bunt bunted that way. Seth and the catcher, Tucker, broke for the ball as Wiley raced toward first; George, with never a thought to linger at third, sped homeward as Tucker and Wendall collided. Tucker was stunned, but Seth grabbed the ball and raced Lukas for home. As the race drew to a close, the hulking figure of Ex was seen very near the plate—to insure, no doubt, that there was no funny business with the tag.

It was close, but as George jogged into the dugout, he took a Panther lead of 1–0 with him. And, more importantly, this misplacement of fielders on Bunt Wiley so confused the Giants that it kept them off stride for the entire three games. With that series sweep the Panthers had accomplished the impossible. They had won the pennant.

The Yankees were a money team then—as they are now—and had breezed their way to the championship. They snickered at the upstart Panthers as their rivals in the Series.

To say that the Panthers were elated to even be in the World Series was the grossest of understatements. But the most delirious of all were Bunt and Ex. They had waited so long and worked so hard for this that they were

just floating—light-headed and giddy—around the diamond in the two-day break between the season and the
Series.

George Lukas, of course, being an ex-Yankee, was
used to this and busied himself with his pitching. Pablo
Sakimoto, who would pitch the first game, was awed by
all the hoopla.

A collision between Tim Starker, the left fielder, and
back-up center fielder Hector Ramirez resulted in a
broken collarbone for Hec. This was unfortunate since
although Hec was rarely ever called on to play the
outfield anymore, he very often pinch hit, either for the
weak-hitting second baseman Martin, or occasionally
when Coach Adams wanted a hitter in Bunt's spot. But,
at least, Tim who was a regular was not hurt, or so he
said.

Opening day of the Series in Panther Stadium came
with much ado, with bands and streamers and shouting,
cheering fans. The radio people made sure to interview
both George Lukas, who had been traded to the Panthers
from the Yankees for Bud Marshall, and Bud himself, to
get their feelings on playing against their old buddies.

But after all the hubbub and after all the introduc-
tions and after the National Anthem, the game finally
began. At this point, Bunt and Ex returned to earth and
Pablo concentrated on his pitching. Bud had informed
the Yankee infield of the most effective ways to play
Bunt, and he was held hitless for the whole day. Pablo
and Stan Miller for the Yankees were pitching brilliantly.
Where Pablo fell short, the Panthers' outfield came spec-

tacularly to the rescue. Harry caught a ball off the bat of third baseman O'Malley that was headed for parts unknown. And Connors Corner saw Ex in two diving lunges that stopped home runs by Bud Marshall and Stan Miller.

No such heroics could stop Ex at the bat. Two of his drives sailed over the Yankee fielders, over Connors Corner, and over Panther Stadium. The papers even claimed they went over the moon. But, wherever they went, one would have been enough as the Panthers won 2–0.

The Yankees, who had been proclaiming they would sweep the Panthers, were embarrassed but attempted to give them a little credit. Pablo Sakimoto was good, they said, but, of course, he did have the hometown fans' frenzied cheering behind him. Harry Webster was good, too, but something of a showboat. And Connors was good, but Bunt Wiley didn't look too threatening.

Game two featured Mike Johnson for the Panthers against Tom Andover for the Yanks. Mike had been the Panthers' steadiest pitcher until George and Pablo were acquired, and still was one of the best.

"Pitch me at home," he told Coach Adams, "and I'll win. I'll give you 50–50 odds at Yankee Stadium." Adams apparently liked the home odds better.

Bunt was more effective going 5 bunts for 5 with an rbi. Again the Panther outfield was superb, and again Connors exploded for two towering home runs. Johnson gave the fans an added bonus pitching the first no hitter in Panther World Series history.

Bunt

At Yankee Stadium, George Lukas started the third game against the Yankees' Paxton. In the first inning Bunt led off with a bunt single followed by a bunt single by third baseman Whittington and a walk to Terry D'Angelo. The first pitch to Connors flew into orbit and the Panthers led 4–0. But then home runs by Marshall, O'Malley, and first baseman Francis in the bottom of the inning closed the gap. The whole game followed suit, and the final score was Yankees, 14, Panthers, 12.

The Yankees were more comfortable with this victory than they had been in Panther-land. Everything had come together for them—except, of course, their pitching—they were rolling now and just see if the Panthers could stop them. To their amazement, however, they split the next two games; and to the amazement of all, Ex had two homers in each.

The Panthers returned home 3–2 ahead of the all-time World Series winners. One more and they had it, but the last could be hard to get. Coach Adams had to juggle the lineup somewhat to get around minor injuries to Starker and Whittington. The new order featured Bunt, Ex, and Harry batting one, two, and three, and although effective, the Yankee hitters matched them easily. Ex again had two home runs and Harry was superb in the outfield, but again, their pitching seemed to abandon them and Game Six ended Yankees 7, Panthers 6.

The media was ecstatic. All the drama they had ever hoped for was here. It all came down to one game at the underdog's park. Could Rookie Sakimoto win such a pressure-packed game? Would the Yankees come through as always and win? And to heighten the suspense, it rained; Panther Stadium turned into a swamp for the day and the final game was played one day late.

Pablo again faced Stan Miller, and both started out in fine form. Bunt had discovered something very important about Miller—he couldn't field. In his first two times at bat he bunted at Miller and was safe at first, but each time that's as far as he got. No one scored until Ex's home run in the fifth. It was not like the other homers; it had just cleared the fence in the shortest part of the park, but it counted. In the seventh, Bud Marshall hit the hardest drive of the game, straight over the center field fence, but Harry crashed violently into the scoreboard as he grabbed it for the out. He crumbled at the base of the scoreboard but was on his feet before Ex got over to him.

"You O.K., kid?" he asked.

"Yeah," he said through his teeth.

"You're not," answered Ex.

"I can make a couple more innings," replied Harry, "I said I was O.K., not great."

"O.K.," smiled Ex, "nice catch."

But leading off the ninth, Bud hit one that no one could catch and the score was tied. Pablo was a little shaken by the blast, but retired O'Malley and Francis. The catcher Rick Trevor hit a ball to left which got away from a limping Tim Starker in the wet grass for a triple. Montgomery was next. Pablo's next pitch was slammed to left center. Harry splashed after it and finally dove just to grab it in the edge of the webbing of his glove. He slid 30 feet to the wall and was covered from head to toe with mud. Ex was again the first one to him, but this time Harry was still on the ground.

"Kid, are you hurt?" he asked with alarm.

"Oh, my ribs!" he said.

"Take it easy," said Ex, "I'll call the doc."

"No, wait," said Harry, getting slowly to his feet, "they'll walk you for sure if they think I'm hurt and we've got no real pinch hitter. I can fake it."

"You're nuts, kid," said Ex, but Harry began to walk slowly in and then for the last few yards jogged to the dugout with a smile on his face.

Martin led off the inning but popped out. Dick Smith pinch hit for Pablo with the same result. As Bunt approached the plate, the infielders shifted here and there. Bunt took the first pitch for a ball. But on the next pitch the unthinkable happened; Bunt didn't bunt, he swung away! He sent the ball deep over the left fielder's head. The Yankee infield turned and watched in amazement. With the traditional Yankee luck, it landed in a mud puddle which prevented it from rolling to the wall, allowing the stunned left fielder to keep Bunt at third.

The Panthers were on their feet half out of the dugout, cheering, shouting, and clapping. Panther Stadium was nearly shaken to the ground by the hysteria in the stands. Stan Miller threw the ball into his glove in disgust.

And now it was Ex's turn. One more home run and he'd be written forever in the record book, he'd be a hero; or he could be the goat. He gazed down at Scotty coaching at third. Scotty had all kinds of signs, signs to hit and signs to take, signs to steal and bunt, and signs to stall. He touched his hat and pulled his nose, he clapped his hands and shook his fist, he flexed his elbow and rubbed his head, and then he did it all in reverse. Ex smiled to himself. That sign meant very simply: walk, get hit by pitch, hit into an error, hit safely or foul off pitches until eternity, but for Pete's sake, man, don't make an out!

Miller knew that Connors needed one more home run for the record and he knew that he would probably get it. In the on deck circle, Harry's heart sank when Miller began to intentionally walk Ex. Harry knew he couldn't hit; he couldn't even hold the bat. As it was, he needed the bat to keep himself propped up where he knelt. This was it, he thought, they'd lost. But Ex wasn't convinced.

"Ball three!" barked the umpire, but on the next pitch Ex took a lazy swing; he missed it by two feet, but he swung just the same.

"Stee-rike!" shouted the ump. Miller and his catcher Rich Trevor stared at Ex in disbelief; the loyal fans stirred anew and the Panther's bench came to their feet. Harry hoped it would work.

Once again Miller pitched the fourth ball and once again Ex took his lazy swing. Miller pounded the ball into his glove as Ex glared out at him. Miller was steaming; he kicked the rosin bag off the mound; he'd love to strike this showboat out. He looked over to the

Yankee bench; walk him came the sign. Bunt knew the sign.

"You've got him now, rag arm! He's scared of the mighty Yankees!" he shouted at Miller. That turned the trick. Nobody dared the Yankees like that; nobody dared *him* like that. He could get one strike on anyone! He looked to the dugout again for the sign. Pitch, it said.

Now Bunt stopped his antics at third and backed up to the bag. The Panther bench held its breath; the fans buzzed in anticipation. Miller wound up and delivered, a sinking curve. Ex couldn't hit that anywhere, he knew. But in the seconds that the ball made its way to the plate, Miller's face twisted in horror—Ex squared to bunt!

At third, O'Malley took a stunned step toward the plate, but he was years late. Ex laid the bat perfectly on the ball; it rolled four feet ahead and stopped. He turned and ran toward first; he ran an inspired run; as fast as any man had ever run. All anybody saw was a streak of white and blue thundering down the first base line. He ran so fast that his brakes failed to stop him at first and he continued down the line and entered full steam Connors Corner from a new angle.

He could have beaten any play or any throw but the Yankees made none. As Connors crashed into the seats, not a Yankee was out of position. O'Malley was still at third and Miller on the mound. Rich was still in a crouch. Ted Francis never moved over to take a throw at first if there had been one. Bunt scored easily; he rounded home and ran down the line to retrieve Ex. He was followed by the other Panthers including Harry and his broken ribs. Ex was clambering out of the seats as they arrived.

"Am I safe?" he puffed, "Did we win?" And although he never heard the answer in the noisy bedlam of the scene, it's certain that he got the message.

Acknowledgments

"The Captain of the Orient Base-Ball Nine" by C. M. Sheldon was originally published in *St. Nicholas* (October 1882). "Marty Brown—Mascot" by Ralph Henry Barbour was originally published in *St. Nicholas* (September 1902). "Hit or Error?" by William Heyliger was originally published in *American Boy* (June 1924). "The Strikeout King" by Franklin Reck was originally published in *American Boy* (August 1932) and is reprinted by permission of Linda Reck Head and Sarah Reck Wakefield. Copyright by Linda Reck Head and Sarah Reck Wakefield. "The Kid from Thomkinsville" (chapters 3 and 4 of *The Kid from Thomkinsville*) by John R. Tunis was originally published in *The Open Road* and is reprinted by permission of Sterling Lord Literistic, Inc. Copyright by Lucy R. Tunis/The Estate of John Tunis. "Opening Day" by Jim Brosnan originally appeared in *Boy's Life* and is reprinted by permission of the author. "Shortstop" by Bill Gutman was originally published in *Boy's Life* (April 1973) and is reprinted by permission of the author. Copyright 1973 by Bill Gutman. "The Game Ball" by A. R. Swinnerton was originally published in *Boy's Life* (April 1979) and is reprinted by permission of the author. Copyright 1979 by A. R. Swinnerton. "Bunt" by Mary Fantina was originally published in *Boy's Life* (October 1980) and is reprinted by permission of the author. Copyright 1980 by Mary Fantina.

Debra A. Dagavarian is the Director of Testing and Assessment at Thomas Edison State College in Trenton, New Jersey. She is the author of *Saying It Ain't So: American Values as Revealed in Children's Baseball Stories, 1880–1950* (1987).